Copyright Notice

IIIIIIIIIIIIIIIIIIIIIIIIIIIIIII
I0549702

© 2020 Crystal Media Communications – B. M. Gage

All rights reserved. Without limiting the rights under copyright reserved above, no part of this publication may be reproduced, stored in, or introduced into a retrieval system, or transmitted, in any form, or by any means (electronic, mechanical, photocopying, recording, or otherwise) without the prior written permission of the copyright owner of this book.

This is a work of fiction. The characters and events that unfold in the work are either products of the author's imagination or are used fictitiously, and any resemblance to actual persons, living or deceased, business establishments, events, locales is entirely coincidental unless otherwise mentioned on the "Author Page" of this book.

ISBN: 978-1-953668-04-2

Author's Note

First, I brought you 'Trapped: Some Stories Are Better Left Untold', and then there was 'No Turning Back', and now we're on 'Trapped: Letting Go'. Man, oh man, we have come a long way since the beginning; can you believe 'Trapped' was released in 2015? Five years later, we are on the third installment.

'Trapped: Letting Go' was written from a place of love and for everyone who was dying to know the fate of Kailyn Green, Samantha Williams, Christina Parker, and the rest of *King Pin*. I felt I'd wrapped it all up with 'No Turning Back', but I received *a lot* of backlash because of the ending. So, I hope 'Letting Go' holds you over...

'Letting Go' is the final chapter in this series... for now. In all honesty, I do this for you. Please leave your feedback and let me know your thoughts on my website and/or the respective Amazon page.

Prologue

Samantha leaned over the casket and wept silently as she saw Kaiden laying.

"Rest easy, baby," she spoke as she touched his chest.

Upon touching Kaiden, she couldn't stop the tears from falling from her eyes.

"I love you," she whispered.

She leaned forward and kissed Kaiden on the lips and felt a tingling sensation run down her spine.

"He can't go!" she shouted.

Samantha woke up to heavy breathing and sweat trickling from her forehead.

She looked to her right and saw the moon shining into the room onto Kailyn.

Samantha rose from the chair and put her hand on the infant to ensure that everything was alright.

She walked to the washroom and threw water on her face. The sound of the water leaving the faucet and hitting the bowl of the sink brought her the peace that she needed.

Samantha turned off the water and dried her face with the towel before turning off the light and exiting the washroom. She walked over and sat down in the chair.

"Is everything okay, babe?" Kaiden asked.

Samantha looked at him and saw him laying down in the bed.

Samantha couldn't help but let a tear fall from her eye.
"Come on back to bed," he whispered with a smile.

Samantha approached the bed. She laid down next to Kaiden and he wrapped his arms around her.

"I had that dream again, baby. I had a dream that you died from the shots Brandon fired," she cried lightly.
"I'm not going anywhere," he kissed her on the cheek.
"I don't want to let go. I'm not ready," Samantha wept.
"You don't have to," he assured her. "Get some rest, babe," Kaiden smiled.

Dedication

I truly want to say thank you for supporting me on this journey. I greatly appreciate your love and support, as it is what motivates me. So many things inspired me to write this piece, including the thought of releasing another work to satisfy you, my fan. I would like to take a moment out to thank my family and friends for their consistent words of motivation, as those also play as factors that keep me moving forward.

As you read this new piece, I ask that you read it, as though you've never known who B.M. Gage is; as though you've never heard my voice before; as though you've never listened to my show and have NO IDEA how I think.

Read it with a new mind. Hey, if you don't know who I am, that's even better; you won't have a bias. All I ask is that you learn more about me by checking me out on The Heat, https://theheatdb.com, following me on Facebook (https://facebook.com/officialbmgage) ad Twitter (https://twitter.com/officialbmgage) and staying up-to-date with my website.

Thank you for taking the time to support me in this journey. This is only the beginning.

https://bmgage.com
-B.M. Gage

1

"Kailyn, baby, come over here," Kaiden spoke to his daughter as she waddled over to him.

Kailyn smiled as her father cheerfully picked her up.
"There's Daddy's little girl," Kaiden kissed her on the cheek.
"These are the memories she will hold on to forever," Samantha smiled as she emerged from the kitchen.

"I know she will," Kaiden spoke with joy. "You wanna go make another hit?" he asked Kailyn.
She squirmed in his arms so that he would put her down.
When Kaiden placed the toddler down, she ran to the stairs and tugged at the door to the studio.

"I'll take that as a 'yes'," Samantha chuckled. "She is truly your daughter," she walked over and sat on Kaiden's lap.
He kissed Samantha on the lips before proceeding.
"She's not just my daughter," he chuckled as he glanced at Kailyn and saw her getting fussy because he wouldn't open the door to go down the stairs. "See that impatience and *spoiledness*, if that's a word," he started, "that's all you."

"Go on and take your diva downstairs," Samantha laughed. "Don't you have Ari coming over in a bit?" she questioned.

"Oh man, I do have her coming," Kaiden remembered as he rose to his feet. "Send her downstairs when she gets here, babe," Kaiden walked to the door.
He picked Kailyn up and walked speedily down the stairs.

Kaiden turned on the lights and powered on the computer. Once the computer started, he powered on the mixing board.
Kailyn sat down in the chair in front of the microphone and spoke unintelligibly.

"When Ari gets here, let's get you to sing a duet with her," Kaiden joked as he typed his password into the system and launched his production environment.
He loaded an instrumental into the program and played it back.

Kailyn clapped her hands together as the music played.
"You like that?" he asked as he put his finger on her cheek.
"*My-my-my,*" Kailyn tried to speak as she touched the object in front of her.
Kaiden assumed she was trying to say microphone.
"My baby girl is talking," he uttered as he adjusted the audio levels on the mixer.
Kailyn smiled and giggled as Kaiden moved her to his lap.
"Daddy loves you," he kissed her on the cheek.

"That's so cute," Ari chuckled.

She put her hair into a ponytail and walked over to Kaiden and Kailyn.

He rose to his feet with Kailyn in his arms and embraced Ari.

"How are you, Kai?" Ari asked as she tickled Kailyn's stomach.

"I'm good, Ari," Kaiden answered as Kailyn giggled. "How about you?"

"I'm pretty good," Ari answered.

"*Ah-wee*," Kailyn spoke as she reached for her.

"Hey!" Ari exclaimed to Kailyn. Ari reached over and took Kailyn from Kaiden.

"So, you're just gonna leave Daddy like that?" Kaiden asked her.

Kailyn looked at Kaiden and felt a little guilty by his question and she quickly reached back for him.

"Uh-uh," Ari scoffed. "You aren't right for that," she spoke to Kaiden.

Kaiden chuckled.

"I'm just playing, baby. You can stay with Ari," he told Kailyn.

Kailyn displayed a confused look and Ari tickled her stomach.

Kailyn laughed and pointed to the microphone.

"You already know what she wants," Kaiden spoke. "She wants you to get in the booth and take her in there with you," he slightly shrugged his shoulders.

Ari looked at Kailyn; the instrumental played on a loop in the background.

"You want me to get on this track?" Ari asked.

"Yeah, I'm thinking of switching things up a bit," he replied as Ari carried Kailyn into the recording studio.

"What do you mean?" Ari asked as she put the headphones on.

"You remember on the tour when I gave the audience the chance to perform?" Kaiden asked.

Kailyn played with the dangling pendant from Ari's necklace.

"Yeah. I can't forget that," Ari chuckled. "They cheered so loudly for the pregnant country singer."

Kaiden nodded his head and gave Ari a look.

"Wait, you're telling me you want to bring her on this track," Ari continued to listen to the track. "It's too urban and *poppish*," she thought.

"That's true," Kaiden started. "But I'm not looking at putting her on this track. I'm thinking about giving this track a Latin vibe or more of a pop feel."

Kaiden adjusted the sliders to increase the bass so that Ari could hear all the downbeats and drums.

"Kai, I don't want to give off the impression of the most conscious or woke person, but you started this company for us."

Kaiden thought about what she was saying.

Ari was right. There weren't too many things that the Black community could call their own, because of the open arms that were always extended to everyone else.

While Kaiden didn't want to create a racial situation, he couldn't ignore the fact that it was about race.

He thought about how if he went into an Arab community, he would see Arab stores. If he went into a Hispanic community, he would see Hispanic stores and restaurants. This was the case for most, if not all, communities — except for the Black community.

"Okay, how about this?" he started. "Why don't we have you on the track by yourself featuring Kailyn, but you change your style up to give it more of that Latin appeal," he suggested.

Ari thought about this.

"It would start a huge buzz," he shrugged his shoulders. "And we can sell it in multiple markets."

Ari adjusted her headphones and repositioned Kailyn on her arms.

"What do you think, Little One?" she asked.

Kailyn looked around the room and reached for the microphone.

Ari laughed.

"I think she's ready to record," Ari spoke over the mic to Kaiden. "Let me see what I can make happen. From the top," she instructed.

Kaiden smiled and restarted the track.
The introduction started and Ari held Kailyn closer to the mic.
Kailyn started to make baby noises into the microphone.
"I think I'm gonna go heartbreak style on this one," she spoke to Kaiden.
"Whatever you want to do, Lil' Mama," Kaiden replied into the channel that wasn't recording.
"I'm going to let Kailyn fool around for a moment, and then we should send her to her mama," Ari suggested. "This track isn't going to be clean," she chuckled.

Kaiden's outlook on his music was different since Kailyn was born. He never recorded any profanity in front of her, although she always wanted to be around him. Instead, when possible, he had his artists record a clean version of their song, that would be sent to radio stations for airplay.

"We'll do two takes," Kaiden suggested. "We'll bring Kailyn down for the radio edit."
"Sounds good," Ari replied.
Ari allowed Kailyn to be close to the microphone and make noises; she would eventually use those in the track as samples and adlibs.
Ari was a little surprised that Kailyn seemed to make the noises almost to the beat of the music.
"This is definitely your daughter," Ari mouthed to Kaiden.
He smiled and shrugged his shoulders.

Ari let Kailyn play and record her vocals for a few minutes before Kaiden called for Samantha to come and get her.

"You all had enough of this diva?" she chuckled as she came down the stairs.

Kaiden kissed Samantha on the cheek before she retrieved the toddler.

"It's only temporary, babe," he assured Samantha. "You know I don't like her around profanity."

"Another reason why you're a great father," Samantha spoke to Kaiden before kissing him on the lips.

"And you're a great and beautiful mother," Kaiden replied.

Samantha gazed into Kaiden's eyes admiringly before speaking again.

"Let me get out of here and let you get back to work, babe," she adjusted Kailyn on her hip.

"I love you," Kaiden reminded her.

"I love you, too," she spoke before walking up the stairs.

Kaiden redirected his attention to Ari.

"All set, Ari?" he asked over the mic.

"Let's do it," she spoke.

Kaiden restarted the instrumental and Ari closed her eyes.

"Ari, Kailyn, let's go.
I was tryna love you, baby
Gave you all my heart
You were never loyal, baby
Messin' with these thots
Kissin' on my lips
Steady whisperin' in my ear
Tellin' me the good shit
You thought I'd wanna hear
But nigga you don't know
Just what that shit has done to me
We breakin' up, I'm leavin' now
It's a fuckin' shame that we
Keep on going back and forth

*Just messin' with my mind
But guess what
Nigga, now I'm walkin' out the door...*"

Kaiden listened to Ari as she continued to flow over the instrumental. He still couldn't believe what he'd put together; the whole platform was astounding and unreal to him, and for him to keep a family-based relationship with his artists while being able to get work done, felt magical.

Kaiden continued to watch Ari as she sang in the booth and couldn't help but imagine Kailyn being on the microphone singing words.

***

"Signed, sealed, and *delivert*," Lester chuckled as he saved the track.

Kaiden emerged from the recording room and regrouped with his team.

"3 tracks in one day has got to be a new record," Byron spoke.

"Well, we're really trying to push these tracks," Kaiden admitted. "Love in the Clouds is almost certified Gold, Hooducated Brotha," he referenced Byron's album, "has gone Gold twice, and we're still working on Lester's debut album."

"So, I guess we're like actual celebrities now," Ari chuckled. "We have to be escorted around, our music is poppin', and can't argue with the fact that we're living the high life."

"But does all of the that determine wealth?" Kaiden asked.

"Ask Uncle Sam, yeah," Byron chuckled.

"Yeah, it brings monetary wealth, but we can't forget the reason all of this was started: to make a difference and bring joy into people's lives. *King Pin* is more than just a brand, it's a lifestyle. We go to these events and we make it happen, by hook or crook. People love us," Kaiden continued.

"Man, all I know is I have had to change my number numerous times," Byron chuckled. "Got groupies hitting me left and right trying to get a taste of this lifestyle."

Kaiden pointed a finger at Byron.

"Keep yours in check, bro," he chuckled. "You don't want to have a Jada on your hands."

Everyone chuckled at Kaiden's joke.

"But on a serious note," he added, "we don't want to be stepping on each other's toes with these hits, so B and Ari, I need for you all to tone it down just a bit," he spoke.

Ari and Byron looked at Kaiden.

"Don't give me that look," Kaiden chuckled. "Lester is our freshman artist, and while he's been on the team for about two-and-a-half years now, we have yet to put out his debut because you two have been producing more than the Octomom," Kaiden cleared his throat. "Which isn't a bad thing, but let's allow Lester to shine. We just finished these tracks, but let's hold back on pushing or promoting them," he finished.

Ari and Byron both agreed. *King Pin* was built on the concept of family; and they each needed a space to shine.

"Well, if that's the case," Byron spoke, "Lester needs to get his ass in the studio and record so we can push more," he concluded.

Lester laughed at Byron and continued.

"I stay in my lane for now," he chuckled. "I know how it is in this game, and I don't want to step on any veterans' toes."

Kaiden shook his head and interrupted.

"Nah, bro, you know how the game goes in Trump's America and the corporate world, but here at *King Pin*, you know we aren't even on that. We're family, and family helps each other."

Ari put her hands together in a praying manner.

"Amen," she spoke.

A few seconds of silence passed.

"Reminds me of **Lilo & Stitch**: Ohana means family; family means nobody gets left behind or forgotten," she patted Lester's shoulder.

"The first thing we need to do is establish a sound for you," Byron suggested. "We can review some of the features and go from there."

Kaiden nodded in agreement.

"Let's do it," Lester finally spoke.

"Let's make history," Kaiden loaded tracks featuring Lester into the system, and the four of them had a listening session.

***

2

Months later, Kaiden and Samantha entered the toddler department of the shopping center and Kailyn ran in front of them.

"Your daughter's a little bow-legged," Kaiden chuckled as Kailyn ran.

"My daughter?" Samantha laughed. "She had to get it from somewhere," she teased.

Kaiden power-walked to catch up to Kailyn and picked her up.

"Yeah, she gets it from her mama," he joked before kissing Kailyn on the cheek.

The toddler laughed as Kaiden held her on his hip.

Samantha rolled her eyes and jokingly pushed Kaiden's shoulder. "Whatever," she laughed.

"You know I love your bow-legged ass," Kaiden continued.

"Uh-huh," she laughed as she thought of a comeback. "I love your psychotic ass too; even with all the groupies," she laughed as she thought about the multiple fans who ran up to get a picture with Kaiden.

She admired Kaiden as both a man and a father. She knew that he was a family man and did whatever he felt was necessary to keep his family safe and protected; but she did fear that he refused to have police officers around when they went out in public, especially after what transpired with Brandon.

But she understood why he didn't have security following him around. Kaiden was a man of the people and loved interacting with his fans. He wore his heart on his sleeve and everyone knew it.

However, if she or the artists were to go out on their own, he had an armed security service he'd built a rapport with to keep them protected.

"Kai-G!" a voice called from behind them.

Kaiden turned around with Kailyn on his hip to see who called his name.

"Oh, damn dog, I didn't know you were with your family right now," the man spoke as Kaiden held Kailyn in one arm and Samantha's hand in the other.

"It's all good, Boss. What's going on?" Kaiden asked.

Samantha realized this was a fan.

"Man, I'm a huge fan," he admitted. "All I do is eat, sleep, and breathe *King Pin*," he chuckled.

"That's love, but you may not want that to be your whole life," Kaiden laughed. "And I'm just another black man trying to make it in America," he adjusted Kailyn on his hip. "So, what can I do for you, bruh?" Kaiden asked.

"Well, yeah man, like I was saying, my dream is to be on the team," he shrugged his shoulders slightly.

Kaiden raised an eyebrow.

"Oh, word?" he asked. "Can you flow?"

Samantha nudged Kaiden slightly.

"Baby come on. We have to finish."

"This will only take a moment, Mrs... G?" the fan couldn't think of her last name.

"This may be good, babe," Kaiden chuckled. "Let's hear him spit a few bars. No profanity in front of my princess, though," he kissed Kailyn on the forehead.

"Right now?!" he asked, surprised.

"The time is now. We aren't promised the next moment in life, so we need to make the most of it," Kaiden spoke.

A chill ran down Samantha's body after he spoke those words.

"Oh crap, okay," the man announced and thought for a second.

"*Chasin' the dollas*
Boy I'm bout my paper
Tryin' to make it in America
You a sucker for later
I was growin' up
I didn't have the keys
Barely had a crib
I had to make ends meet
This world already ain't fair
If you black in this country
Man, it just don't mix
System is designed to shoot first, ask later
Man, I hate this ish,*" he remembered that Kaiden didn't want profanity.

"*Tell me how am I to grow*
When no one knows
How it goes
When you're black with the flows
And your pants hang low
You're not trying to perpetu-
Ate the stereotype of a black man
Runnin' late
Sellin' dope and poppin' off
But it's all you know..."

Kaiden listened to the fan rap and nodded along.
He could use some work on delivery and the lyrics weren't top-
notch, but Kaiden understood what he was trying to convey and
understood that everyone had to start somewhere.

"I didn't come here
To hurt nobody
Or bring no issue
But if you got a problem
Or are messing with me for fun
Don't bring it here
Nah I don't have no gun, I'm not gon' front
But these words will kill you."

Kaiden thought for a second before speaking.
"What'd you say your name was?" Kaiden asked.
"Bishop," he replied. "I would give you my rap name, but I don't
need one," he chuckled.
"Bishop," Kaiden started, "how old are you?"
"I'm 22," he replied.
Kaiden chuckled at Bishop.

"I'm not gonna lie; that was alright," he started. "You could use a
little work, but tell you what, take down my email and shoot me
your track. If it's hot, I'll invite you to come to *The Base.*"
"Oh man, that's love bro," Bishop replied.
Kaiden gave Bishop his email.
"Keep grindin', kid," Kaiden spoke. "And get me that track."
"I got you," Bishop shook Kaiden's hand.
"Byeeee!" Kailyn shouted as Bishop walked away.
Samantha and Kaiden both chuckled.

"Just another brother trying to make it in this country," Kaiden
shrugged.

"And, this is another reason why I love you," Samantha spoke as she touched Kailyn's hair. "You're always providing opportunities."

"Someone's got to," Kaiden finished as he put his arm around Samantha, and they continued their shopping. "No one else will."
***

"What y'all thinking?" Kaiden asked his team when the song finished playing.

Lester was the first to speak.

"I mean, he has the potential," he admitted.

"It's a whole lot of something," Byron spoke. "Where'd you find this cat, Kai?"

"He approached us while Samantha and I were out shopping," he chuckled. "I see potential in the homie," Kaiden spoke.

"Yeah, he has potential," Byron spoke.

"But can he build on that?" Ari answered.

"I think it's worth it," Lester replied. "Give him a chance."

"We're still waiting for you to break out," Byron laughed.

"Oh, mine is coming," Lester replied. "Just wait on it," he sipped his water.

Kaiden was truly trying to determine whether to bring Bishop on board.

While he saw potential in Bishop, he knew he couldn't make a business investment and pour all the money into an artist who wasn't producing anything; he was living through it with Lester.

"Kai," Ari spoke interrupting his thoughts, "can I see you outside for a second?" she asked.

"Everything good?" he asked in reply.

"I just need to speak with you for a minute," she insisted in a low tone.

"Okay," he spoke. "Smoove and Prophet, I want for you all to think about the pros and cons of bringing this man on board," he instructed. "We'll make a final determination in a moment."

"Got it," Byron replied.

Ari led the way up the stairs and away from the studio; Kaiden followed her.

"What's going on?" Kaiden asked as they walked outside of his home.

"I gotta be honest with you, Kai," Ari started. "I don't know if you should devote the energy to this new guy," she admitted.

"And why is that?" Kaiden was curious.

"Because it's an extra investment and I'm truly not sure if we can afford it at the moment," Ari opened up. "Kai, I know you. When you see potential in someone, you go all in to bring it out of them. Throwing them on the tours, including them as features on singles, and putting your all into it. The label is already living through it with Lester, and I'm not sure if this new guy will be another Lester or will come in hitting the ground running," she finished.

Kaiden thought about everything she was saying. Coincidentally, these were thoughts that were running through his mind about bringing Bishop on.

"Well, let's leave the financials to Samantha. That's her thing," Kaiden chuckled, "but I get what you're saying. I was just thinking about the same thing, but how about we bring him in on a trial?" Kaiden suggested.

Part of him really wanted to see what Bishop could do and what magic could potentially be made.

"And as far as Lester, that's why I'm asking for you and Smoove to pull back a bit. I want to see what he can do," Kaiden spoke. "You all have had the spotlight forever," he laughed, "so let's see what the rookie can do."

Ari nodded her head in agreement.

"You sure about this?" she asked.

"Well, let's go see what Byron and Lester say, and then we'll make a final determination. Like we always say, *King Pin* is built on family, so it has to be a mutual agreement."

Kaiden and Ari reentered the home and walked down to the studio. They reentered the studio.
Byron and Lester were finishing their notes as Bishop's song was ending.
"So, what are the results?" Kaiden asked. "Is it a go or no-go?"
"If you see the potential in him and think he can go far," Byron spoke, "take that chance. It's a go from me."
Kaiden nodded his head.

"What about you, Prophet?" Ari chuckled.
"More talent means more money," he laughed. "If you think he has what it takes, let's do it."
"And you, Ari?" Kaiden asked.
She shrugged her shoulders.
"Go for it," she chuckled.
Kaiden clapped his hands together once.
"Alright then. Ari, baby girl, give Bishop a call and let him know to come through in two weeks at about 1:30. Give us time to do what we gotta do."
"AM or PM?" Ari jokingly asked.
"If he comes through in the AM hour, he gettin' popped," Kaiden laughed. "I'm about to go speak to Samantha and Kailyn for a minute." Kaiden exited the studio and walked upstairs.

As he opened the heavy soundproof door that separated the home from the stairs to the studio, he heard a familiar voice playing with Kailyn.
For a moment, he thought his mind was playing tricks on him; there was no way that Isaias was here in Chicago.
He turned the corner and saw Christina, Trequan, and Isaias in his living room talking to Samantha and playing with Kailyn.

"*Daa-yee*," Kailyn spoke excitedly as she saw her father and ran over to him.

He bent down and picked her up and kissed her on the cheek.

He placed her back down as Isaias walked over to him.

Isaias gave Kaiden a high-five.

"Hey, Kaiden!" Isaias spoke.

"What's going on, little man?" Kaiden asked.

He looked up and spoke to Christina and Trequan.

"What's good Tina? Tre?"

"What's good, bro?" Trequan asked as he gave Kaiden a handshake. "How you been?"

"Doin' the damn thing," Kaiden spoke. "Getting to this money," he laughed.

Christina couldn't help but shed a tear as she saw Kaiden.

He'd saved her son's life, and there was no way she felt that she could ever repay him. Even after everything they'd been through, he was willing to risk his life for her son.

She rose to her feet, walked over, and embraced him.

She silently wept.

"Hey there," Kaiden whispered to her. "What did I tell you? You don't have to cry. I told you, I would always be here to watch over everything and make sure everything was smooth," he started.

Samantha got goosebumps hearing him speak the way he was.

"We are like a family," Kaiden chuckled. "A weird and dysfunctional family, but a family none-the-less," he finished as he hugged Christina.

"You just don't understand how grateful I am," she spoke. "My son could have died that day," she added as they both retreated from the hug.

"Don't even talk like that," Kaiden replied. "No one is going anywhere. We're all going to be right here," he smiled.

Christina couldn't help but smile at Kaiden. He had a contagious spirit and could always lighten up the mood.

"Speaking of which," he continued. "What brings you all here?" he asked.

"We're moving here," Isaias blurted.

Kaiden quickly turned his head to Christina.
"Washington just isn't cutting it anymore," she responded. "I want to start over with my life, and we're going to do that here in Chicago."
Kaiden displayed a concerned look.
"That's the big news," Samantha spoke with a smile that Kaiden perceived to be phony.
Kaiden widened his eyes at her but didn't exchange any words in front of Christina or Trequan.
Samantha made a face at him.
"What about work? What's going to happen?" Kaiden asked Trequan.
"I got a position down here," Trequan replied. "Same company; they were just able to transfer me," he cleared his throat. "Moving wasn't in my plans and isn't my first choice, but it's the way things work themselves out," he added. "Plus, we already know people here, so why not?" he chuckled.

Christina walked back over to the couch and Kaiden walked into the kitchen with Samantha.
"Well, I'm happy for you," Kaiden remained optimistic and kept a smile about the situation. "You all are going to be just fine," he poured himself a little bit of Hennessey into the red cup.
"It's even better because we're moving about 10 minutes away from you guys."
Kaiden nearly choked on his drink once Christina spoke.
"Shit, this stuff is hot," he tried to play it off.

"Baby, be careful," Samantha replied as she patted him on the back.
"It's all good, babe," he spoke.
A few moments of silence passed before another word was spoken.

"You all down there making magic?" Christina asked to break the silence.

"Yep, we are," Kaiden answered. "Speaking of which," he drank the rest of the Hennessey from the cup, "I gotta get back down there."

Kaiden put the cup down and kissed Samantha on the cheek. "Be back in a bit," he called out.

"Go on and kill them, babe," Samantha spoke as he disappeared behind the door.

Kaiden reentered the studio and saw Lester with a notepad in front of him with lyrics.

"Kai, let me murder a track," he spoke confidently. "Smoove has been playing this one on repeat, and the music spoke to me. I got the perfect hit," he concluded.

"This man is ready to make music," Kaiden chuckled to Ari and Byron. "Let's hear you work," he added. "Get in the booth."

Lester walked into the booth and put on the headphones.

Kaiden made eye contact with him through the glass and spoke over the microphone.

"You set?"

"Let's do it," Lester confidently projected.

Kaiden started the instrumental and Lester began to rap. Kaiden's phone vibrated twice and he checked it.

> *Samantha: Tina and Tre left. Isaias is still here, but I want to talk to you about this when you get a moment.*

Kaiden replied to Samantha's text.

> *Kaiden: I know. I am not fond of the idea of her living right around the corner, babe, but we can talk about it. We should be done soon.*
>
> *Samantha: this shit doesn't sit well with me. -_-*

Kaiden: it doesn't sit well with me either, baby. I'm not too comfortable with her living around the corner with the way she's acted, but what are we going to do lol?
Kaiden: want me to send Smoove to take her out?
Samantha: you're stupid lmao. No, don't do that. Idk.... We will talk about it baby.
Kaiden: it'll be fine. Let me finish making these million-dollar records ;)

Kaiden returned his phone to his pockets and Lester was finishing his rap.

"Bossin' up and fightin' hard
Keepin' it all subtle
This new nigga just ruined your whole career
There's no need for a rebuttal," Lester breathed heavily into the microphone.
"You good?" Kaiden asked.
Lester continued to breathe heavily.
"Let me hear that back," Lester spoke over the microphone.
"Playback," Kaiden spoke as Ari restarted the track for listening.
Lester, Ari, Kaiden, and Byron all nodded their head to the beat of the music.
Kaiden felt his phone vibrate and he retrieved it from his pocket.

Christina: Is it another hit?

Kaiden looked around before replying.

Kaiden: It is.

He returned his phone to his pocket and continued to nod his head to the music.

As the track ended, Byron spoke.

"I think you did it," he congratulated Lester. "The track to put you on the map."

Ari nodded her head in agreement.

"I remember the track that got me started with *King Pin*. "***A-R-I L-O-V-E*,**" she remembered as she turned in the chair. "Remember that, Kai?"

"How could I forget? That beat and hook are still in my head," he sang a lyric from her song. "*I'm doing this not for the fame or the money. My first name is Ari, middle name is silent, last name L-O-V-E.*"

"I think we all remember our first single," Byron spoke. "Mine was a hip-hop joint that had all of the parties bouncin'," Byron stated, "***A Smoove Jam.***"

"Don't I know it," Kaiden laughed. "That was when I was just starting out as well."

"I would say that I remember my first single, but it's too fresh not to remember it," Lester laughed.

"Don't worry. We're going to push this out and get you some recognition," Kaiden expressed.

"And now, we're kicking back and watching as the fans scream our names," Ari laughed.

"The fans are our family too," Kaiden suggested. "We couldn't be where are without them."

"That's true," Ari replied.

3

Ari sat on the porch with an ice-cold bottle of water as she watched Kailyn play with her toys on the lawn.

Kaiden and Samantha were in the home discussing the move for Christina and plans.

Kailyn brought Ari the toy before multiple black suburban trucks sped and came to a hard stop in front of the house.

Multiple people emerged from the vehicles and began speaking.

"This is *The Base*," the woman spoke aloud.

"Tear it all up," one of the men spoke as they approached the home.

Ari quickly picked up Kailyn and held the child close to her.

"Hold up," she spoke. "What's going on?" Ari questioned.

"Mam, stand back," the woman spoke as she approached Ari. "We have reason to believe there's illegal activity going on in the home," she showed Ari her badge and the search warrant.

The men walked up the steps; Kaiden and Samantha walked towards the door after witnessing the commotion.
All the officers aimed their weapons at the two as they emerged from the home.
"What's going on?" Kaiden asked with his hands up, remaining calm for Kailyn. He didn't want her to see him riled up.
"Kaiden Green," the woman announced, "Officer Riley," she introduced herself. "We have a search warrant to search your home, a-k-a '*The Base*'," she finished.
Kaiden looked at a copy of the warrant.
"I'll say this," he stated while reviewing the warrant, "whatever you all take out, you better handle everything with care. If *anything* ends up broken, I'm taking badge numbers and going straight to the city for this unlawful ass search," he finished.
"What 'suspicions' do you all have?" Byron asked.
"An anonymous tip," Officer Riley answered.
Police officers entered the home and walked past Byron.
"There isn't a damn thing illegal about black people makin' music," Lester defended.
"Lester, calm down," Kaiden spoke as he recalled his past interactions with police. "Let them make a fool of themselves," he chuckled. "They're just wasting time," he made eye contact with Officer Riley.
"*The Base* is in the basement of the building. Search the entire structure," she smirked as she finished over the radio.

"Alright, *King Pin*, huddle up," Kaiden announced to his artists and they crowded around.
"What's up, Kai?" Ari asked.
"Let's make sure 12 doesn't plant anything," he directed. "I want someone in *every* room that they go in, especially *The Base*. Smoove, you take *The Base*. Ari, you take upstairs where the

bedrooms are and Lester, take the first floor. The doors are all locked, and if they need entry, which they probably will, tell them to come to me for the codes," he instructed.

The artists nodded their heads.

"Lock it down," Kaiden finished.

Ari passed Kailyn over to Kaiden and entered the home alongside Byron and Lester.

Kaiden eyed the officers as they entered the home.

Samantha put her hands on Kaiden's chest.

"Why do you think they're here?" she asked.

"Someone called them," Kaiden responded. "The question is, who?"

"We have no reason to be worried, though," Samantha responded.

"I hope that's a statement and not a question," Kaiden uttered as he put his hand in Kailyn's hair.

"Now, why would I ask something like that?" Samantha placed her lips on his.

As they retreated from the kiss, Kaiden spoke again.

"I know better than to do anything to jeopardize you or Kailyn. My job is to protect, and that's what I will *always* do," he smiled.

Samantha shuddered a bit at his comment but kept her hand on his chest and embraced him.

***

"Damn, Kai. Can't seem to catch a break," James spoke over the microphone. "More cops?" he chuckled.

"They hate to see a black man shine," Kaiden shook his head lightly and chuckled. "But, as these cops can see, my hands are clean."

James laughed.

"So, tell me," he smirked, "what was all of this about?" he pressed play on the screen and a fan-recorded video of the police raid played.

"I've never even seen this video," Kaiden admitted. "Now that I'm seeing it from a third person's point of view, me and the team were definitely set up."
"An ex?" James asked.

Kaiden thought about how Christina came to the house days before the raid and told them that she was moving nearby.
No, she couldn't have been the culprit. She wouldn't do that to him, her best friend, or their child.
He then thought about Jada and how silent she had been since the *No Turning Back* tour.
"There could be one person responsible for it," Kaiden addressed. "And I'm not going to blast her name, but just know that I see you," he laughed.

James laughed along with Kaiden.
"Use it as motivation," he responded. "You're on the rise, man. Your music is bumpin', your artists add life to everything they touch, and your production is phenomenal; it can't be touched."
"That's love, man, thanks," Kaiden replied.
"There seems to be a theme across *K.P.*," James spoke, "especially when there's a social injustice going on. Many others and I admire you and your crew for that."
"Respect, Boss," Kaiden started. "But I don't know how many times we can keep saying the same thing," he laughed. "America isn't going to change. Hell, now we have to worry about Karen calling the cops on us for having a damn barbecue," he chuckled.
James nodded his head in agreement.
"I get what you're saying, and I couldn't agree more," James continued. "America is in a fucked-up state right now."
"Ever since Agent Orange got into office, America has been wildin' and showing its true colors."
"Man, tell me about it," James shook his head. "You got people mad about Kaepernick taking a knee during the national anthem to protest police brutality but didn't say shit when Tebow took a knee to protest abortion. He was hailed as a hero while

Kaepernick is being blackballed and is said to be disrespecting the flag."

"America, the beautiful," Kaiden chuckled. "Maybe this is the way people have always been, and since Trump got into office, they feel comfortable showing their true colors. But let someone try that shit with me or mine. Shit, *bi-bink*," Kaiden laughed.

"What's even more messed up is that people are more upset at Kaepernick for taking a knee than they are at these white folks for shooting up these schools. This shit happens on a regular now."

Kaiden shook his head.

"Fuck it, Kailyn is getting homeschooled. If something were to happen to her, me and Sam aren't going to be on the news crying, we're going to be on the news with a mugshot because someone is going down for it. I don't play that shit," Kaiden shook his head. "How the hell do we live in a country that's so busy trying to keep immigrants out because of 'fear' of terrorism, but they still haven't realized that the real threat is already here in the country?" Kaiden's fire was being fueled. "My brothers are out here dying and being arrested for no damn reason, but you got the damn colonizers getting a slap on the wrist. My nigga Sammy Grier got arrested and charged with committing an act of terrorism for walking into a mall with a fake gun, but then you got Becky with the good hair who was able to carry an AR-10 to her graduation, and nothing happened to her."

Kaiden made eye contact with Samantha and paused.

"Look, man, all I'm saying is this, we demand equality. There's no way in hell all these school shooters and mass murderers can get arrested without a single scratch, but then my brothers are out here getting beat on for not wearing a seatbelt. How long do they think we're going to take this shit? We're not just going to remain seated and voiceless. It's only a matter of time before we revolt," he finished.

"Revolt, huh?" James asked. "Aye, Quest, put that beat on."

The DJ started the instrumental at a low volume, slowly increasing the audio level, and James continued.

"Putting you on the spot," he told Kaiden. "Show them that Kai-G can still deliver, even though you haven't dropped your own track in months," he chuckled.

"Nah man, I'll pass," he spoke to James.

"Don't tell me that Kai-G is backing out of a challenge."

Kaiden planned it out.

"Nah bro, it's not even like that, but it's not my time to shine," he responded.

"Don't be a chicken," James taunted.

"Is that what you think?" Kaiden asked. "Kai-G ain't scared of nothing," Kaiden spoke.

He rapped on the downbeat.

"Picture this: there's blood on the wall
It's scary
Got brothers teachin' the word
Like missionaries
Done faced so much shit
Shit you probably won't see
We in two different places
But you gon' notice me
You live in Hinsdale
Nigga, I live in the C
Yeah, y'all play so many games
But know, you can't play me
Nah I don't have to stunt
You don't see no fear in my eyes
May have been born in Bart
But Chi-town till I die
I keep my head up
And keep prayin' for my niggas
They wanna see you fail, struggle and die
Hah, it figures
Another black man from the city
The city don't care

They say 'if you can make it here
You can make it anywhere'
But that shit's not true
Bump it, this shit is hard
Mama out there hustlin'
Just so that I could get far
Now I'm not here to complain
And say that it's all bad
But I'm from where you from
A dollar is all I had
Mamas crying, babies dying
Shit, just my luck
Go to the mayor
That nigga just don't give a fuck
She's a cluck
Or maybe she's just new to the game
But Mayor L, there's a war going on
Time to step to the plate
Too much blood shed
That's that Jim Crow shit
We try to help each other
But it's hard to quit
Yeah, I know how it is
You gotta move the way you move
You gotta eat the way you eat
You gotta chew the way you chew
Kai-G, muthafucka
I'm keepin shit trill
Never had to kill, but fuck with me and mine
You gonna have to feel this steel
Brothas killin' each other
This shit is hard to stand
Talked to moms the other day
I had to hold her hand
And let her know
I'm not going nowhere

Mama, please don't cry
I can promise you this
Kaiden Green won't ever die
Don't let go
Just keep holding on for dear life
It might take me a minute
But Ma, Imma make this right
This legacy I'm making
I rock this shit on my chest
Well, I didn't say shit
But you know, it's for the best
Got my niggas
Smoove and Lest rockin' out
Ari, Sam, Kailyn
That's what it's about
King Pin till I go
Shit is hard to predict
Now, I'm not foreshadowing shit
But that's just what it is
My niggas, we gotta make a change
It all starts with us
Look at the dollar bill
Shit says, 'In God we trust'", the DJ cut the beat to the track and
Kaiden continued to rap acapella.

'Cause, hey, when it's all said and done
My niggas gon' have the last laugh
Meditatin', contemplatin'
Let's live life fast
This a quick message to my niggas: Don't stop dreamin'
And don't stop believin'
You can and will bring a change
Shit, my eyes can see it," Kaiden flowed and James interrupted.
"My brother, Kai-G," he hyped him up as the DJ played an air horn
sound effect.

Kaiden was still in rap mode but quickly came back down to Earth as Samantha touched his hand.

"That's how you deliver," James reached over and clapped hands with Kaiden.

"Kai-G, ladies and gentlemen," he spoke over the microphone as he played the 'cheers & applause' sound effect.

James continued once the sound effect ended.

"I see you bring this beauty with you everywhere you go," he referenced Samantha.

"This is my rock," Kaiden spoke with a smile as he looked at Samantha. "She's always there for me," he continued.

"And that's how love should be," James spoke. "It's all about supporting one another through the good and the bad times."

"You know what they say in marriage," Kaiden started, "to have and to hold for better or worse, for richer or poorer, in sickness and in health, till death do we part," he kissed her on the cheek.

Samantha smiled and put her arm around Kaiden.

"Nothing but love in the studio right now," James continued. "But I gotta ask about the little one. How is she?" he asked.

"She's doing well," Kaiden answered. "With the sitter right now. I didn't want to bring her here," Kaiden chuckled. "She would have a field day with all of this equipment."

"You keep that little girl busy, don't you?" James asked.

"She wouldn't be a Green if she didn't get started early," he slightly shrugged his shoulders.

"Well, you know we got nothing but love for you, *King Pin*, and the Greens up here," James stated.

"And that's why I rock with you, bro."

***

"Kai, can you come here for a minute?" Samantha called out.

Kaiden sat in the room with Kailyn watching television.

"Is it urgent?" he joked as he rose to his feet.

"If you enjoy having all of your limbs, it is," Samantha laughed as Kaiden walked into the kitchen.

Kaiden walked up to her and kissed her on the lips.

"What's up, babe?" he smiled.

Samantha put her hands on his chest and sighed.

"I think you'll want to see this," she spoke as she showed him her phone.

Kaiden read the phone and the headline on the page.

DJ Lexington Fires Shots at Kai-G, Kailyn, & King Pin

Kaiden pressed play on the video and listened to the entertainment news story.

"*In the rap game, beef seems to be the oxygen to the bloodstream. There's a new beef that's started. DJ Lexington of T.K. Nation has fired shots at King Pin and on the track, he's fired shots at the head of the coalition, Kai-G, as well as his daughter.*"

"Is this nigga serious?" Kaiden spoke aloud as the video played.

"Babe, who is *T.K.* Nation?" Samantha asked.

"Eddy," Kaiden shook his head in disgust. "My homeboy Eddy; he started up a label after I let him go from *King Pin*, and he's operating under the name of DJ Lexington."

"I remember him," Samantha spoke as she shook her head. "Didn't know he was operating under this new name."

The video continued.

"*I know Kai-G personally,*" Eddy spoke to the camera. "*So, for him to act all holier than thou is beyond me. But it's only beef. However, remember to choose your fights wisely, children,*" he chuckled.

The camera went back to the reporter.

"*DJ Lexington has released 'Who's The King' earlier today, and with lines such as 'who am I to beef with a nigga with a kid?/fuckin' with his girl's best friend, ay, that's some bitch nigga shit', and 'Ridin' my dick to get a show/ We came and conquered, and now I pulled out, but you still a hoe', it's evident that DJ Lexington is not here for the games.*"

"Turn that shit off, babe," Kaiden spoke as he shook his head.

Samantha pressed the home button on her phone and returned it to her pocket.

"Let me text this fool," Kaiden pulled out his phone and texted Eddy.

Kaiden: Who's the King, huh?

To Kaiden's surprise, Eddy replied almost immediately.

Eddy: lol

Kaiden didn't expect much of a reply from Eddy during this. He knew how he would have to handle Eddy, and it wasn't going to be pretty.

Kaiden: if this is what you want, say that shit and I can send it. but keep my daughter's name out your mouth
Eddy: lol

"This nigga is playing games," he spoke to Samantha.
She didn't like to see Kaiden worked up, so she stood behind him and hugged his waist.
"Calm down, baby," she comforted him.
"You're right, babe," Kaiden spoke. "I'm not going to feed into the negativity."
Kaiden interlocked his fingers with hers.
"As long as he keeps your name and Kailyn's name out of his mouth, it will all be good," Kaiden warned.
"I hope he gets the message," Samantha kissed Kaiden's cheek before they left the kitchen.

The two of them entered the room with Kailyn and Kaiden laid on the floor beside his daughter.
He put his hand in her hair and his thoughts were soon interrupted by an incoming text.

Byron: Kai, we got smoke?

Kaiden couldn't help but laugh at the text.
Kaiden immediately received another text after Byron texted.

Ari: You got a story for me?

Kaiden knew they were both referring to the incident with Eddy.
He sent a group text to Ari, Byron, and Lester to inform them of
the next steps to take.

*Kaiden: I could have sworn he wasn't a problem, but I see he is
going to be. Let's make sure Bishop is on board with King Pin, and
let's focus on doing us. We rise above all this foolishness and let
shit go. We gonna be the bigger people; let our work speak for
itself*
Ari: You sure that's how we're gonna handle it?
Lester: I'm sleep
*Byron: mmhmm. You know we could end his whole label right
now*
Kaiden: that's what he wants. We're gonna rise above
*Lester: there's a fire burning, and the fans are waiting on a reply
from K.P... The question is: what are we going to do?*
*Kaiden: we keep doing what we've been doing. We can't let him
take us out of our element*
Ari: let me know what you need from me, Kai

Kaiden shook his head at the group thread.

Kaiden: DO NOT RESPOND TO TK Nation, guys.

"Sam, I have an idea," Kaiden spoke.
"What's up, babe?" she asked as she ran her fingers through
Kailyn's hair.
Kaiden rose to his feet.

"I know you're not a singer, but baby, you have a voice on you!" he exclaimed.

"Don't tell me you're thinking about me getting on the mic," she laughed.

Kaiden chuckled.

"Babe let's do a duet," he spoke.

Samantha was confused as to where this idea came from.

"And why the instantaneous idea?" she asked.

"I'm just sitting here admiring your beauty, and the idea came to me. *King Pin* isn't known for duets, so to have one featuring the head of the label would be genius."

Samantha thought about what Kaiden was saying.

It could draw a ton of buzz to the label, and it would take *King Pin*'s focus off of the Eddy situation, but she wondered why he didn't just team up with Ari to do it, considering she was actually on the label.

"And don't even ask," Kaiden chuckled, "I mean, I could ask Ari to do the track with me, but our chemistry would be much stronger," he chuckled.

"Get out of my head, Kai," Samantha laughed. "How did you know I was thinking that?"

"I know everything about you," he laughed. "I know what you're thinking and feeling."

Samantha laughed heartily at his idea.

She wasn't a singer and Kaiden knew this. She could sing well and was told she had the voice of an angel, but not once did she ever truly think about recording a song.

But it was with Kaiden; her husband and the man she was madly in love with.

"Write the lyrics, and we'll see," she chuckled as she walked closer to Kaiden.

"I love you," he spoke as he discreetly grabbed her butt.

"Kailyn is right there," Samantha blushed.

"She's not even paying attention," he kissed her lips.

"I love you, too," she blushed and smiled.

"*Daa-yee*," Kailyn called to her father.

The show she was watching ended and Netflix was asking if they were still watching.

"My name is *Dad-dee*, little girl," Kaiden enunciated and joked as he walked over to her.

Kailyn rolled her eyes.

"*Daa-yee*," she repeated with a laugh.

"That's it," Kaiden spoke and laid Kailyn on her back.

He blew into her stomach and tickled her; she started laughing uncontrollably.

"Children, please," Samantha joked with Kaiden. "Let's not forget Tina, Quan, and Isaias are coming by tomorrow. We gotta go straighten up," she spoke.

It still bothered her that Christina decided to move around the corner from them, but she was slowly accepting it.

She couldn't tell her to leave the city and go back home; who was she to tell someone where to go?

Kaiden chuckled.

"It's not even anything to clean," he smiled. "Shit, make her do the cooking since she wants to come over so badly."

"That's not how any of this works," Samantha responded with a slight laugh. "Come on, Lazy," she walked to the door.

"Your mama's buggin'," Kaiden spoke to Kailyn.

Kailyn displayed a disapproving look.

"I heard that," Samantha called.

"You were supposed to," Kaiden immediately replied.

4

"Where is King Pin?" The media outlet reporter asked. *"Not even 24 hours have passed, and we have yet another tracked dropped by T.K. Nation, titled '4 Shots'; making references to the incident that happened on the first stop of the 'No Turning Back' tour to Kai-G."*

Kaiden was in the studio working on lyrics for the duet that he wanted to record, and Kailyn was with Mama Green.
Samantha knew that Kaiden wouldn't be interested in hearing about the drama that Eddy was trying to create, but Samantha was curious to hear the track, so she clicked on the link under the video.

The instrumental to the song started and Samantha knew it wasn't anything nice. The beat was produced by Eddy and had a very dark sound to it.
She listened to the rap.

"Yeah
T.K Nation
DJ Lexington on the beat

They wasn't ready for this one.
Kai-G, Ari, Smoove, King Pin. Yeah, y'all niggas got 24 hours.
Just 24
Haha
I didn't want to do it, but you made me"

Eddy was warming up to deliver the track and Samantha shook her head.

"*Hey Kailyn, hey Sam,*" he chuckled before the rap started.
"*Come battle me nigga, let's go one on one*
Lexington's at your head so you better go run
Or cry like a bitch, 'cause my lyrics'll hurt you
I'll take your bitch, fuck her, then give her back to you
I'm runnin' this game, my shit is tip-top
You thinkin' you winnin', my nigga just stop
You sinnin' and lyin' like livin' in Eden
Like 'No Turning Back', I'll leave yo ass bleedin'
Got shot in your hip, the rib and the thigh
With that shot to the lung, how did you survive?
I'm comin' for blood, if it's yours, I'mma have it
Fuck that kid you protectin', nigga, you ain't the daddy?"

Samantha shook her head as the track continued.
"Hearing this shit, you would think Kaiden really did something to this man," she spoke aloud.
She felt goosebumps as he rapped about what happened after the tour, and anger filled her body.

"*Call my ass Brandon 'cause I'm here for murder*
You lovin' his child, bruh you need to stop hurtin'
The kid is not yours, now go check on Kailyn
You sendin' me texts but you sittin' there brainless
Go handle your business and quit wastin' time
Bitch Pin goin' to shit, and I'm comin' for mine
We airin' shit out, and I don't give a fuck

If you say one mo' word, then you shit out of luck
That spiritual shit that you on is just wack
Nigga, you in it, there's no turning back
The moment that you just decided to spite me
You talkin' mad shit but I bet you won't fight me
These are some problems you'd rather not have
Get tested for Kailyn, I might be the dad
Let me stop lyin', I won't fuck with that
'Cause if I'm fuckin' Samantha, I might get the clap
Let's move to Christina, and Quan and Isaias
This shit ain't a joke, do you see what I'm sayin'
Keep it contained and I'll keep it movin'
Psych, I'm just playing. Where's Ari and Smoove at?
And Lester the Prophet, my nigga, just stop it
I bet when it drops, man, that shit'll be floppin'
I'm speakin' the truth, but you don't wanna hear it
I got the crown now and you ain't comin' near it
Demons exposed and the truth is revealed
T.K. takin' over, come get this steel
Kai-G, Ari Love, B. fuckin' Smoove
Lester, my nigga, I got all the tools
My niggas, we savage, we kill your whole team
Keep playin' this track and you'll find out what I mean
We started this shit when we were just shorties
But look at you now; fuckin' actin' all holy
This shit is for fun and I eat you for dinner
I spit yo' ass out, now you know I'm the winner
This beat is just flowin', I keep on rappin'
it was money over bitches, what the fuck happened?
I'm just gon' say that you done sold yo soul
To make a quick buck, man this shit's getting old
You thought y'all in love, till the story got told
You found out the truth, man that bitch was so cold
Was breakin' yo heart, you ain't see it comin'
Had you screamin' for a minute, 'fuck bitches get money'."
Eddy laughed and continued.

"King Pin is a joke; y'all niggas ain't with it
These secrets revealed, now they know who the king is."

"Yeah," Eddy laughed over the instrumental, *"and this is only the beginning. Like I said, King Pin, y'all niggas got 24 hours."*

She picked up Kaiden's phone and called Eddy. He answered on the first ring.

"DJ Lexington," he answered.

"Eddy, what the fuck is the problem?" she asked.

"What you mean?" he asked.

Samantha could tell he was smirking.

"Get that damn smirk off your face," she replied. "You are lucky as shit that Kaiden hasn't heard that track yet."

"I helped Kaiden launch *King Pin*; technically, fifty percent of K.P. belongs to me," Eddy asserted.

"Eddy, you knew the game when you did that foul shit to Kai," Samantha defended Kaiden's decision to move Eddy out of the label.

"He wasn't saying that shit when I was bringing in the money," Eddy continued. "Nah, everything was damn near perfect then," he chuckled. "Like I said, *King Pin* has 24 hours to respond, or else," he threatened.

"Or else?" Samantha questioned.

"You'll see," Eddy hung up the phone.

Samantha was disgusted at how childish Eddy was acting and how low he was stooping. She was wondering if anyone from *King Pin* had heard the diss.

Her phone vibrated and she checked the text.

Christina: wtf!

Samantha knew that she must have been referring to the track.

Samantha: don't come over and alert Kaiden. He doesn't need the stress.

Samantha locked her phone and walked down to the studio with Kaiden.
She stood behind him and put her arms around him.
Kaiden looked behind him and smiled when he saw Samantha.
"How's my baby?" she asked.
"Working hard, baby," Kaiden spoke. "I want to make sure the lyrics are perfect for this duet we're going to do," he spoke.
"Why don't you get Ari to help you write it?" Samantha questioned as she tried to stay away from the conversation about the diss track.
"I mean, I could," he responded, "but I'd have to see her first," he chuckled. "Speaking of which, let me try to call her," Kaiden spoke as he felt his pockets for his phone.

Samantha retrieved the phone from her pocket.
"You left it upstairs, babe," she handed it to Kaiden.
"Thanks, babe," Kaiden spoke as he unlocked his phone.
A text from Eddy came through.

Eddy: 23hrs and 50minutes

Kaiden was confused at the text.
"Fuck," Samantha whispered.
"What, babe?" Kaiden asked her.
Samantha sighed and opened to Kaiden.
"Eddy dropped another diss track," she confessed. "I didn't want for you to stress over it or get upset," she shook her head.
"This nigga's really busy, huh?" Kaiden chuckled. "Well, I know he's not causing any major fires with the tiny matches he has."
Samantha shook her head in disapproval.
Kaiden's smirk left his face.
"Really?" he asked.

Samantha stood in front of the keyboard and put the address of the website into the browser.
Kaiden watched the video first and then he listened to the track.

"Wow," Kaiden spoke once the track ended. "This man has dropped bombs on everything, not to mention he's trash-talking you and Kailyn all throughout the track."
Samantha could see anger boiling within Kaiden.
"I just told this nigga to keep your names out of his mouth, and he just smothered the tracks with your names," Kaiden chuckled as he clenched his fists. "And these accusations," Kaiden chuckled, "he's really asking for it."

Kaiden rose from his chair and paced the floor.
"Baby don't get all worked up over this," she explained.
"Nah, baby, I'm good," Kaiden chuckled as he rested his fists.
Samantha walked closer to Kaiden and held his hands.
"I don't want for you to do something to jeopardize everything that you've built and worked for," she spoke.
"Babe," Kaiden started, "it's just a little rap beef. The nigga is still butthurt that *King Pin* is taking over and *T.K. Nation* is still struggling to get off the ground," Kaiden looked at the computer screen. "Weak ass nigga."

Kaiden and Samantha's conversation was interrupted by the sound of the doorbell.
He pressed the button on the mixer and turned on the monitor and saw the camera outside of their home.
Ari, Byron, and Lester waited at the door. It was rare for Kaiden to see all three of them arrive at the same time, especially if it was an unannounced arrival.
Kaiden pressed and held the microphone button and spoke.

"Come on in, y'all. I'm in the studio."
Kaiden pressed the button under the desk and buzzed the door open.

The three entered the home and walked into the studio.

"Who the fuck is DJ Lexington?" Byron asked with a chuckle as they arrived downstairs.

"Well, hello to you too," Kaiden laughed as he clapped hands with Byron.

"Man, you done pissed him off," Byron laughed. "Homie is hurt."

Lester clapped hands with Kaiden as Ari hugged Samantha.

"He sent shots at everyone back to back; didn't even give us a chance to respond."

"He just wants attention," Kaiden spoke as Ari approached him. "He wants a reply to get his clout up," he hugged Ari.

"What's up with him?" Lester asked, "and how does he know so much about us?"

Kaiden thought about the time when things were good with Eddy.

"Eddy, or 'Lexington', used to be part of *King Pin*," Kaiden sat back down next to Samantha. "When I first started the label, Eddy was truly my partner-in-crime, in terms of launching K.P. Smoove, you remember my very first show?"

Byron thought back to *The Big Showdown* at the All-State Arena.

"Yes sir. That was my first performance," Byron replied.

"Yeah," Kaiden continued "Eddy set that up. So, I cut him a good percentage of proceeds," Kaiden spoke.

"So, why is he bitchin'?" Lester asked.

Kaiden held Samantha's hand and continued.

"Eddy did some foul shit and I kicked him out of *King Pin*. He didn't do anything in terms of music and production for the label, so I didn't even worry about him trying to be petty on that. But this nigga feels entitled," Kaiden laughed. "Saying how he wants 50% of the company because he feels like he helped put the company together."

Ari chuckled.

"Better tell his ass to move around," Ari announced.

Lester raised an eyebrow.

"So, why so much anger in the last track? I mean, he went a little personal, and you don't seem upset at all," Lester added.

"Because I'm in a place where I don't feel any of this anger," Kaiden smiled. "I want for him to let all of his anger out and get the attention he wants. I'm going to reply, but make him wait for it," he chuckled.

Byron gave him a look.

"Unless y'all trying to record me right now," Kaiden joked.

"Just you?" Byron asked.

"This is a personal beef," Kaiden replied. "It's not even just rap. He was saying shit about my previous relationship, what happened after the NTB tour, threw allegations on my wife's name, *and* he dissed all of us here at *King Pin*," Kaiden responded. "Not to mention, this fatherless bastard included my daughter in his rap, even after I told him to leave her and Samantha out of it. If he has a problem, settle it with me."

"You did not just call that man a fatherless bastard," Samantha laughed.

"I did," Kaiden lightly laughed. "He wants to get personal, we can."

Kaiden loaded an audio track into the system.

"You know this shit is all over social media. It's the talk of the world," Lester spoke as he scrolled through his phone.

Kaiden pulled out his phone and looked at some of the comments about the track.

"The fans are going wild," Kaiden spoke as he read. "Some of them are even calling me a bitch for not acknowledging it."

"Get in the booth then," Byron spoke. "Shit, or I'll do it for you. He came for the whole team and we're just sitting back taking it."

Kaiden thought for a moment.

"Before we do that, let's load up his track, and let's pick it apart. I have hella shit on Eddy, so me replying won't be an issue, but I'm going to do it K.P. style," Kaiden said.

***

5

"So, Kai-G has finally replied," the host spoke. "What's going on, everybody? I'm your boy, Benzo, in for Cool J, and you are listening to 'Uncut Double X-L'. I'm sitting here with DJ Lexington and the artists from *T.K.* Nation."

"What's up?" Eddy spoke over the microphone.

As Kaiden listened to the radio in the studio with Samantha, Ari, Byron, and Lester, he could hear that Eddy was under the influence of something, based on the tone of his voice and the way he was slurring his words.

"Man, you are fuckin' lit," Benzo laughed. "What'd you take? Slide me some of that shit," he chuckled.

"Shit, man, I did some acid and can't go wrong with the weed," Eddy laughed.

"You give no fucks, huh?" Benzo asked.

"You damn right like I give no fucks about what Kai-G has replied with."

"Well you know the shit dropped yesterday," he reminded him.

"A full week after I dropped two tracks. *Bitch Pin* isn't on shit," Eddy put his hands on the table. "Let me hear that bullshit," he told Benzo.

"We'll get to that," Benzo shuffled through papers, "but before we do that, introduce who you brought with you and the role they play in *T.K. Nation*."

"Shit, everyone has a voice," Eddy chuckled. "I brought three artists that I manage with me. Didn't bring my bitch though; I don't take mine everywhere I go," he fired a shot at Kaiden. "But y'all go on and introduce yourselves."

"This nigga is petty," Kaiden laughed at the statement. "I'll let him live though. He just wants attention; let's let him shine," he spoke to the group.

Eddy's first artist spoke.

"What's good everyone?" a gruff voice asked. "I go by Hurricane. Shit, I joined *T.K. Nation* about a year ago, and it's one of the best moves I've made in a while," he spoke as though it were rehearsed.

"They treatin' you right over there?" Benzo asked.

"No doubt. Me and Lexington are some killers when it comes to this music. Name a better producer," Damian spoke over the microphone. "I'll wait."

Benzo laughed.

"So, what role did you play in these tracks?" Benzo referenced **4 Shots** and **Who's the King**.

"Nah, that was all Lexington," Damian chuckled. "Shit, I wish I had his genius."

Damian looked at the next artist.

"Hey guys, I'm Jada, a-k-a Luscious Jade. *T.K.* Nation became part of my life about three years ago. I came across Lexington and found out that he delivers on his word."

"You're a rapper, aren't you?" Benzo asked.

"That's the only way to roll. How you gonna have heavy ass rappers on a label and throw in an R&B singer?" Jada spoke cunningly.

"This man really went out and scouted out people who have played a negative role in your life," Samantha shook her head.
"Let him live and have his fun, babe," Kaiden calmly spoke.
Samantha admired how Kaiden was handling the whole ordeal; she loved how he well he handled negative situations.

"I'm the latest addition to *T.K.* Nation," the final artist spoke.
Kaiden's eyes widened a bit when he heard the voice.
"My name is Bishop. It goes both ways," he laughed. "I use it as my stage name and it's my birth name."
"That's a blessing," Benzo spoke.

"Bro, what the fuck?" Byron asked.
"Weren't you looking to get this nigga?" Lester asked. "What the fuck happened?"
"Y'all know I didn't get an answer," Ari replied. "I guess we know why."
Kaiden smiled and gently spoke.
"Guys don't worry about it. He's a free spirit and has the right to go wherever his heart desires," he chuckled. "We're going to keep doing what we have to do."
Ari and Byron looked at each other as they all continued to listen to the interview.
"Where's Cool J?" Byron asked inquisitively.
"Not sure," Kaiden spoke as he pulled out his phone to text James.

Kaiden: Yo, you good?

James replied almost instantly.

James: they wanted me to interview Lexington and I couldn't do that shit.
James: I'm on your side and I couldn't sit in that studio and interview someone who was going to trash your name
James: so I took a personal day.
Kaiden: Nothin but love and respect to you bro.

"Cool J said he didn't go in, because he's on our team. He couldn't interview someone who was going to bash us," he announced to his team.

Kaiden returned his attention to the interview with the rest of his team.

"I think y'all should play that shit," Eddy laughed. "Let the world hear that whack shit."

Benzo laughed and started the instrumental to Kaiden's reply. "Alright y'all, here's the awaited reply from Kai-G. It's called **Still the King**. Right here on Double X-L."

Benzo started the track and Kaiden increased the volume.

"*Lexington, you know you fucked up, right?*" Kaiden spoke over the track. "*The moment you decided to put Samantha, Kailyn, and all of King Pin in your shit.*"

Kaiden chuckled on the song.

"*This shit is personal, handle it with me,*" he continued to speak. "*But, since we're airing shit out, I want to give a special shoutout to T.K. Nation for the free pub. K.P.'s Album sales have tripled since your release. Guess we know who the king really is.*"

Kaiden inhaled on the song and started the rap.

"*Listen closely my nigga*
You put my girl up in your song
I could be mad, but I'd just rather rap along
This shit is scary
I thought this shit was dead and buried
You made me do it, just know my shit is legendary
Yeah, it's true, we started this when we were kids
I'm grown up now, just look and see how I live
While in this biz, I can't seem to control this shit
Money, power, fame, respect, and all that comes with it."

Kaiden remembered looking at a picture of he, Kailyn, and Samantha when rapping this part of the song, and it immediately took him back to the recording booth.

"We started hot, with all these words that I be spittin'
You on the beat, metaphorically that shit was crippin'
I saw your vision, and we looked at how they livin'
I wanted to give the children something to believe in
But then you changed, you got caught up with the fame
You played the game, and acted like you knew a thang
It stayed the same, I pushed and fought while you remained
Kept your eye on the fame, shit we couldn't grow that way
You had your chance, to show you were the man
It was a plan, but you wanted to keep that stance
You fuckin' punk, bruh, know that I'm doing what I can
To keep you afloat with those weak ass jams
I can't work with a nigga that complain
Yo shit been floppin', and you need someone to blame
So, you drop a diss track, but you should think and contemplate
How I'm gon' retaliate, nah nigga, I'm just playin'
See Samantha and Kailyn and Ari and Smoove
And Lester, the Prophet, we got all the moves
We keep on movin' and bendin' the rules
We don't need a diss track to compete with you fools
But since this is the place you've longed for and yearned
Let's sit with the fans; Lex, will you confirm
How you couldn't cope and decided to turn
To the drugs and lean, man, shit started to burn
You turned to the weed, and the X, and the pills
To the meth, and the coke, nah, nigga, just keep it real
There's a reason you couldn't succeed with K.P.
All the hurdles you brought, man that shit was draining
Since we're telling all, what about Jada and Dame
Y'all want it so bad, you'll do anything for fame
Including bashing a nigga who's on top of his game
I'd wish you the best, Jade, but go drown in your pain

Man, that was harsh, trust I'm gonna get checked
I'm having this pain that I will not neglect
I'm having this damn urge to rap and perfect
Rapping's my gift and you gonna respect
This ain't what I do, I did it for fun
The next time you name drop, you better go run
Run hard, run fast, nah let me not front
I'll kill you with skill, bitch, my word is my gun
You want one-on-one, my nigga come at me
Say 'Kailyn' again and you'll have to combat me
You cannot succeed or even distract me
You'll have to come harder to win in this rap beef," Kaiden
finished rapping and spoke over the instrumental to the song.

*"So, do me a favor bruh. Keep King Pin out your fuckin' mouth,
a'ight? Don't let me hear you mention Sam or Kailyn again, or I
will be at your front door and we gonna have some words. You
got beef, fuck with me. You wanted to go one-on-one, right? Live
by your word,"* Kaiden recited the outro to the rap aloud to his
team.

"Ladies and gentlemen, we are back. Live on the air with DJ
Lexington and *T.K.* Nation right now," Benzo spoke as the track
ended. "So, Lexington, you gotta tell us how you're feeling about
that track."
Eddy cleared his throat over the mic.
"It was cute," he chuckled. "But I expected him to drop some hot
shit," he explained.
Kaiden could hear Eddy take a sip of whatever he was drinking.
"Not that weak-ass diss."

"I don't know, man," Benzo spoke. "That threat didn't seem like it
was meant to be taken lightly," he chuckled. "Kai-G sounded
pissed."
"Kaiden Bryson Green can be as pissed as he wants to be," Eddy
laughed. "The world needed to know the truth."

Benzo laughed as well as the members of *T.K.* Nation.
"So, be real for a second. Was the part about you potentially being Kailyn's father real? Did you really fuck Samantha?"
Eddy scratched his beard.
"Whatever I said I did, I did that shit," Eddy chuckled. "I'm no show pony."

Kaiden kept a smile on his face.
Ari, Byron, and Lester all had looks of shock on their faces.
"It's not true," she whispered as she put her hands on Kaiden's.
Kaiden allowed her to rest her hand on his.

"I just got a quick message," Eddy spoke. "Kaiden, I know you're listening. I had to let people know the truth. I started this *King Pin* shit, and I'm not going away," Eddy looked at his team as he spoke. "I want half."

Kaiden powered off the mixer, which turned off the radio.

After a few moments of silence, Kaiden spoke.
"Everyone, get out for a moment," he calmly spoke.
"Kai, what's our next move?" Ari asked.
"I know you aren't going to let this go unanswered," Byron replied.
"Yo, it's all good," Kaiden replied. "I'll hit y'all up in a bit," he directed them to the door.
King Pin didn't say a word; they left the studio.
Kaiden and Samantha waited downstairs.
Once he saw them leave the home, he spoke.

"What is Eddy talking about?" Kaiden asked. "He's stuck on this idea that Kailyn is his."
He felt his heart sink to his stomach.
"Kai, Eddy is lying," Samantha spoke. "The only times I've been around Eddy were with you. And you know that," she explained.

"Why is he on this run? The more he says it, honestly, the more it's messing with me," he said.

"Eddy is on bullshit, Kai. Don't let him get in your head." She softened her tone. "I love you, and I wouldn't do anything to hurt you, babe."

Kaiden's hurt turned into anger, but he wasn't sure if it was anger at Samantha or anger at Eddy. He wanted to believe Samantha, but because of what happened with Christina in the past, it was hard to do so.

"This shit is happening all over again," Kaiden spoke as he became dizzy.

He punched the wall and fell to his knees.

"Kai," Samantha walked over to him and kneeled.

She tried to comfort him.

Samantha's heart sunk as she saw Kaiden like this. He was hurt and it was coming out.

"You know I would never do anything to hurt you," Samantha assured him.

"Yeah, and I also know you're Christina's best friend; and you are who you associate with," Kaiden spoke as he rose to his feet.

Samantha knew he was recalling the incident with Christina and Jordan, but it hurt her that he associated her with Christina's actions.

"Wow," she spoke in shock, "so you're really going to go there?" she asked with a few tears in her eyes.

"It's the truth. She was a cheating and manipulative woman, and you associated with her, so I can't be sure if you approve of it or not," Kaiden paused and took a breath of air. "Even when she was cheating, you didn't outright tell me. I had to find that shit out for myself," he finished.

"You know me, Kaiden," Samantha spoke, taking offense. "Why in the hell would I be with you to put you through the same thing? You know precisely how I feel about you and I wouldn't do that to you."

"Says every girl who gets with a big-time star."

"You think I'm with you for money?" Samantha raised her tone. "Kaiden you can keep the money. Trust me, I can make my own shit. I'm with you because I love you."
Kaiden shook his head.
"I can't believe you're gonna believe the shit that Eddy's saying over your fucking wife. I've been at your side through thick and thin: when Christina fucked you over, when Jada came with her bullshit, when Brandon came through and tried to kill you, when all of these allegations came out against you, it was me. I was there!" Samantha's hurt was quickly turning into anger.
Kaiden didn't reply. The hurt was too deep, and the pain was too familiar.

Samantha took off her necklace and rings.
"I don't need your fucking money, Kai. That's not why I'm with you. And I'm not with you for Kailyn either. Shit, if I wanted you for money, I could put you on child support."

Samantha left the studio with tears in her eyes. Kaiden shortly followed her and walked upstairs.
She walked into their room and pulled out her phone and texted Christina.

Samantha: Thanks a lot

She returned her phone to her pocket and pulled a suitcase from the closet.
"I'm gonna take a moment to myself," she spoke to Kaiden as she began to put clothes in the suitcase.
"Whatever you need to do, do it. I don't care," Kaiden shrugged his shoulders.
Samantha chuckled in disbelief.
"You have a good woman in front of you, but you're choosing to believe someone who doesn't give three shits about you, over her," she shook her head as she referred to herself in the third person. She continued to pack.

She removed her credit card from her pocket and placed it on the dresser.

"Just so you know I don't need your money," she shook her head. "And Kailyn's coming with me."

She knew that would hurt Kaiden, but she didn't care. She wanted him to experience pain the same way she was.

Her phone vibrated as she started her exit, and she pulled it out.

Christina: for what?
Samantha: for breaking Kaiden. He's so damaged that he's willing to believe what Eddy is saying over me

Kaiden shook his head.

"Where the fuck do you think you're going with my daughter?" he asked.

"Her mom's leaving, so she's going as well," Samantha spoke before laughing lightly. "Plus, didn't Eddy say she may be his, even though we *never* had any kind of physical contact other than a handshake?" she shook her head. "Don't worry; you'll still get to see her."

Samantha closed the suitcase and walked past Kaiden.

"Excuse me," she spoke as she carried the suitcase down the stairs.

Kaiden was conflicted. He knew that Samantha loved him but based on his past, he didn't know who to trust.

He wanted to say something to stop her, but he couldn't fix his face to say anything; his pride wouldn't let him.

Samantha opened the door and pulled out her phone.

Christina: what do you mean?
Samantha: we're arguing. I'm leaving and taking time for myself.
Christina: damn, girl.
Christina: I'm sorry
Christina: do you want to stay with us?
Samantha: fuck no lol. You've done enough

Samantha closed her texts and opened her Uber application. She requested a car.

"Where are you going to go with my daughter?" Kaiden repeated. "Don't worry about it," Samantha spoke. "Like I said, you'll still see her."

A driver arrived for Samantha. The car was a metallic black color and Kaiden heard the brakes squeak as the car came to a stop. "Samantha?" the driver called as he lowered the window. Samantha looked at Kaiden. "Question for you: why is it that you're choosing to get upset now, but you didn't when you first heard the track?" Samantha raised an eyebrow. Kaiden didn't reply. He put his hands in his pocket. "Something to ponder on," she finished before walking from the porch.

Samantha walked to the car and the driver exited the vehicle. The driver took her suitcase and put it in the trunk. He opened Samantha's door and she got inside of the vehicle. He closed the door and looked at Kaiden.

"Oh shit, it's Kai-G," he spoke with excitement. Kaiden ignored the fan and walked back into the home. "Damn, did I offend?" the driver asked aloud as he got back in the car. "It's just this whole thing with DJ Lexington that's messing with his head," Samantha spoke to the driver. "I don't know why I didn't put two and two together when I accepted this ride," he replied. "You're his wife." "I am," she answered. "Why are you requesting an Uber?" he asked as he drove away. "I 'm pretty sure you all have some nice whips you could choose from," the driver chuckled.

"Can we not discuss that?" she asked politely.

"I'm sorry," he apologized.

He looked in his rearview mirror and noticed Samantha looking out of the window and wiping a few tears from her eyes.

He knew the two must have had an argument or something of that nature, and he felt a little resentment.

He tapped a button within his Uber application and canceled the ride.

After Uber confirmed the ride was successfully canceled, he spoke.

"Samantha, I'm going to need that address again. My app just tweaked," he lied.

"Yeah, the app just told me the ride was canceled," Samantha addressed.

However, she didn't think twice about giving him the address again.

"Thank you, Mrs. Green."

The driver went offline on the app and continued the drive in silence.

An hour later, the driver arrived at the home and opened Samantha's door before retrieving her suitcase from the trunk.

"The ride was on me," the driver confessed. "You're going to get a notice that it was canceled, but Uber isn't going to take any money from you for it."

"Now, why would you do that?" Samantha asked softly as she opened her purse.

The driver held her hand down to stop her from giving him any money.

"It was my pleasure to drive you. I hope you have a better day, Mrs. Green," he spoke.

"Thank you," she gave him a quick embrace.

He walked back to his car and drove off.

Samantha walked to the door and rang the bell.

The door opened and Kailyn spoke.

"Mommy!" she shouted. "Granny, Mommy's here," she informed her grandmother.

Mama Green walked to the door.

"Yes, she is," she spoke. She looked down and saw the suitcase. "Samantha, what's going on?" she asked.

"Mama, Kailyn, and I need a place to stay," Samantha still had tears in her eyes.

"Come on in, baby," she unlocked the security door and held it open for Samantha.

Samantha walked into the home and took her suitcase to the bedroom.

Mama Green followed Samantha to the bedroom.

Samantha turned around and hugged her.

"Tell me what's going on," Mama Green spoke.

"Kaiden and I had a fight," Samantha started as she continued the hug.

"Baby don't tell me he kicked you out," Mama Green interrupted.

"No, Mama," Samantha replied. "I left."

Mama Green walked Samantha over to the bed and took a seat on the edge.

"What's the problem?" she wiped Samantha's tears with her hand.

Samantha sniffled but managed to explain the situation to her mother-in-law.

"It all started with this beef with Eddy," Samantha started. "In his rap, he put something about how he had sex with me and how Kailyn may not be Kaiden's," she shook her head.

Mama Green also shook her head.

"Now, I know that's not true," Mama Green replied. "You love my son and I know you wouldn't do anything like that."

"Kaiden was cool with the name dropping but then Eddy had this interview, and I guess it messed with Kaiden's head."

"Maybe I need to give Eddy a call," Mama Green suggested as she picked up the phone.

"No, Mama, don't do that. It's a rap beef; it has to be settled between them."

"I'm not trying to end up like Tupac or Biggie's mothers; I don't want to lose my son to this rap thing."

"I don't think it's that deep, Mama. I think Eddy's scrambling to stay relevant." Samantha pulled the bedsheets back. "Kaiden wasn't going to reply until Eddy pretty much pressured him to do so."

Mama Green put her hand on Samantha's shoulder.

"Sam, I love my baby boy so much, but you and I both know what happened in his past with Christina,"

"I know, Mama. I just hate that he won't believe his own wife over a snake-ass person like Eddy," Samantha was disgusted.

Samantha rose to her feet and opened her suitcase.

She began to unpack, and Mama Green spoke again.

"Are you hiding?" she asked.

Samantha took a pause and looked at Mama Green.

"Mama, I'm not hiding," she chuckled. "I just need some time away from Kaiden," she continued unpacking the clothes. "Maybe then he'll realize what he has," she mumbled.

Kailyn entered the room and saw her mother unpacking the clothes.

"What are you doing, Mommy?" she asked. "Where's *Daa-yee*?"

Mama Green looked at Samantha.

Samantha looked down at Kailyn and spoke.

"Daddy's being stupid, baby, so we're going to stay here with Granny for a while."

6

"Lester, you've got to deliver!" Kaiden spoke over the microphone. "For every one track we lay, Eddy is finishing up three," he stressed.

The rap beef between Eddy and Kaiden continued and while Eddy seemed to find amusement in the ordeal, Kaiden was stressing and it was showing.
"Find that hurt and deliver that pain," Kaiden emphasized.

Lester shook his head; he knew what was upsetting Kaiden.
Lester cleared his throat.
"Run it back," he enunciated.
Kaiden repositioned the cursor and started the recording again.
As Lester rapped, Kaiden looked at his phone.

Eddy: Why da fuck you buggin? lol it don't have to go down lyk dis.
Kaiden: bro, we gonna keep this in the music. I'm not giving you half of my company. That shit's dead

*Kaiden: I tried doing business with you, and it was a dead
mission. You sweatin' me ain't doing shit
Eddy: lol you really wanna do this?*

Kaiden ignored the final text and put the phone down and Lester
was finishing his rap.
"Let's take a break," Kaiden announced over the microphone
when Lester finished.
Lester removed the headphones and exited the recording booth.

"How was that take?" Lester asked as he sat down in the chair.
"I'm sorry for spazzing out on you, bro," Kaiden apologized. "This
shit with Eddy is on my mind and Samantha and Kailyn not being
here is fucking me up even more."
"I get it, man," Lester spoke. "And plus, this is my first album, so I
know you want it to be perfect. Hell, I want it to be perfect."
"You're repping *King Pin*, man. We all want it to be perfect. It's
just that this shit with Lexington is fucking with me. He's been
irrelevant for years now, and suddenly, he wants to come back
and the first thing he does is attack me and mine."
Lester put a hand on Kaiden's shoulder.
"We got your back," he assured Kaiden. "I'm going to do what I
can to ensure this is a hit and we're gonna knock Lexington's
irrelevant ass off the map."
Kaiden clapped hands with Lester.

Lester pulled out his phone and opened his Twitter app.
The first tweet he saw on his timeline was about Jada.

*@EntertainmentLikeYesterday: TK Nation's Luscious Jade Attacks
King Pin's Kai-G in latest track, I Was There.*

A link was included with the tweet.
Lester tapped on it and it took him to a YouTube video.
"Bro," Lester announced with a headshake. "Check this out," he
showed the phone to Kaiden.

Kaiden looked at the device.

"Let's load this up on the monitor," Kaiden announced as he typed the link into the web browser.

The instrumental started and Kaiden increased the volume.

"Kaiden — I mean Kai-G, this is just going to tell the truth. I'm not dissin' or clout chasin', but before you start telling these lies, I'm gonna let the people know what really went down," Jada spoke over the instrumental.

"Player, how you gonna act like you don't care
When you know I was the one that was there
When she tore you to pieces and left you to bleed, yeah yeah
I know that shit just wasn't fair
Mmmm
Wakin' up in the mid of night
Havin' dreams that didn't seem so right
Kissin' me but still thinkin' 'bout her
And had the nerve to be so uptight
I was there
Yeah-yeah
I was there," Jada sung.

"She could definitely use some work lyrically," Kaiden chuckled. Lester laughed as they continued to listen.

"When we got together, you was around the town
I met you shoppin' for 'The Big Showdown'
'Kaiden Green', nigga, you threw it on the card
You had them bags, man you was livin' large
I didn't know you then, didn't know who you were
When you were doin' the show, you up and rocked my nerves
Man, that shit was classic, I'm not gon' even lie
Rappin' that fire shit, I was so surprised
I was there for you.
Yeah, yeah
I was there

When she just sat and lied
And brought tears to your eyes
Made you want to die, nearly committed suicide
I was there."
Jada continued to rap over the instrumental, but Kaiden lowered the volume.

"This is what I'm talking about," he explained to Lester. "Eddy is hard at work to destroy my name."

"Yeah, but this shit is rushed," Lester added. "Granted, the beat is sick, but her delivery isn't there. We don't have anything to worry about when he's putting out tracks like this."

"I just don't like the fact that he's putting my personal life out there," Kaiden spoke. "And it's not just one or two areas; they're airing *everything.*"

"Put it like this," Lester rose to his feet. "If they're airing your dirt, they're airing their own lives. You would think they know about you by now."

Kaiden chuckled at Lester and closed Jada's track.

"I'm not even going to stress over it," Kaiden laughed. "She's just about to dig her own grave and end her career before it gets started."

Kaiden looked at the time on the computer and checked his phone.

"Any word from Sam yet?" Lester asked.

"Nope, just Christina," Kaiden shook his head.

> *Christina: we need to talk*
> *Kaiden: about what?*
> *Christina: you and my girl.*

Kaiden sighed with relief. He thought she was going to say something about the two of them.

Kaiden: well, I'm working with an artist right now. But I'll hit you up when I'm done. Maybe you can come through and we'll discuss it over dinner or something lol

Christina was no stranger to Kaiden, and he no longer felt the need to pretend like she was. His feelings for her were gone, so he believed, and he hoped that hers were as well, but he couldn't be too certain.

Every time their bodies connected, it seemed to bring flashbacks of their relationship to his mind; the good parts of the relationship.

He didn't know if inviting her over for dinner was the right call, but he wanted to focus on letting the hurt go.

Christina: lol yeah right. Well let me know when would be best for you

Kaiden locked his screen and looked at Lester.
"Let's finish this masterpiece."
■■■
"Mama, do you know where Kailyn's favorite shoes are?"
Samantha asked as she finished putting Kailyn's hair into two afro puffs.
"I don't know, Sam," Mama Green replied. "Check in the pantry," she called as she put the final dishes away.
Samantha kissed Kailyn on the forehead and walked to the pantry and retrieved the shoes.
Samantha walked into the kitchen.

"Have you heard from my baby?" she asked.
Mama Green looked at Samantha and rolled her eyes with a slight chuckle.
"You mean *my* baby?" she asked.
"I *deebo'd* him. I mean, it's kind of like he's both of ours,"
Samantha laughed and touched Mama Green's shoulders.
Mama Green shook her head.

"No, baby," she lightly laughed. "Not today I haven't. He told me yesterday that he had some work with one of his artists. What's his name?" she tried to remember. "Fester, Hester…"

"Lester," Samantha corrected her with a laugh.

"That's the one," she chuckled as she put a pan on the stove. "You know he is always working."

"What he needs to work on is his trust in me and our marriage," Samantha spoke in a low tone.

She was disappointed that Kaiden didn't show that he trusted her, because of what happened with Christina.

Samantha would never do that to Kaiden, but she didn't know how to make him understand.

Mama Green looked at Samantha.

"Come here, baby," she spoke as she sat at the table.

Samantha sat next to her.

"How much do you love my baby?" she asked.

Samantha raised an eyebrow.

"More than anything, Mama," she explained. "You know that."

"I know that," Mama Green started, "but does *he* know that? Have you ever given him a reason to question or doubt you?"

Samantha understood where Mama Green was coming from; not only as Kaiden's mom but as a woman.

"No, I haven't," Samantha answered. "But Christina has," she shook her head.

"And you think he's using that against you?" she asked.

"I know he is," Samantha played with her fingers. "Kaiden has insecurities, Mama, I know that. And so, I'm trying to help him through them, but he can't if he can't let Christina's mistakes go."

"I'll talk to him, baby," Mama Green assured her.

"Thanks, Mama," Samantha reached over and took Mama Green's hands.

"Don't worry about a thing. If it's one thing I know, it's that my son really loves you, Samantha. Right now, as much as you're thinking about him, he's thinking about you."

"You think so?" Samantha asked.

"I know so," she answered. "Kaiden is a sweet boy and if anyone knows his heart, it's me," Mama Green chuckled.

Samantha smiled.

"Just leave it up to me and God," she stroked Samantha's hand. "Everything will work out."

"Thanks, Mama," Samantha responded.

"Now go on and get my grandbaby ready," she chuckled. "Come here, Kailyn," Mama Green called.

Kailyn walked into the room and Samantha chuckled at the sound of her feet hitting the floor.

It sounded as though she were running.

"Yes, Granny," she walked over to Mama Green.

She chuckled at Kailyn's hair.

"I know you are not about to send my grandbaby out here like this," she joked with Samantha.

"She's adorable," Samantha laughed. "What's wrong with her little puff balls?"

Mama Green shook her head with a slight laugh as she put Kailyn on her lap.

"Besides, we're just going to meet with Ari," Samantha added as she rose from the chair to put on Kailyn's shoes.

"What are you all meeting with her about?" Mama Green asked.

"We're just going to hang out," Samantha addressed. "Going to crunch a few numbers, discuss the future of *King Pin*, and just do girl stuff afterward."

Mama Green put Kailyn on the floor and rose to her feet.

"Well," she began, "if it's involving money, make sure you keep me in the loop," she chuckled. "These bills don't pay themselves," a smirk formed on her face.

"I know," Samantha laughed.

She looked at her phone after it vibrated.

Ari: I'm outside

"Mama, she's here," Samantha spoke as she rose to her feet and embraced her mother-in-law.

"You all stay safe and keep a low profile," she mentioned as she finished her embrace with Samantha.

"We will, Ma," Samantha added.

Kailyn hugged her grandmother and held her mother's hand.

"Bye, Granny," she called.

"I'll see you soon, Kai-Kai," Mama Green replied as Samantha and Kailyn exited the home.

Samantha exited the gate and walked to Ari's car. She opened the back door and Kailyn climbed inside.

"Hey *Ah-wee*," Kailyn spoke as she put on her seatbelt.

"Hey Kailyn," Ari replied with a smile to the toddler.

"Hey Ari," Samantha sat in the front seat and embraced Ari.

"How you doin', Sam?" Ari greeted her as she pulled away from the home.

"You know me," Samantha replied. "Doing what I gotta do for me and my daughter. How about you?"

Ari put on her turn signal and merged onto the expressway.

"I'm doing cool," she uttered. "Helping Lester with what he needs to finish pushing his album."

"How's it coming along?" Samantha asked.

"That's top-secret, girl," Ari joked.

"You must forget that I handle the books for *King Pin*," Samantha laughed.

"I'm joking," Ari chuckled. "He's almost finished. I think he and your man were working on it earlier today."

Samantha rolled her eyes at Ari's comment and Ari noticed this.

"You all still not speaking?" Ari asked.

"Haven't heard from him," Samantha twiddled her fingers.

Ari put her hand on Samantha's shoulder as she drove.

"I'll be real with you," she began. "You are *all* Kaiden speaks about. So, don't think that he doesn't care, because he really does." Hearing this made Samantha smile, but she didn't allow her smile to be seen.

"That's cool," Samantha stated.

Ari scoffed at Samantha's gesture.

"Don't act like you don't care," she shook her head as she read through Samantha's expression.

Samantha looked at Ari.

"Don't act like you know me," she chuckled.

"Better than you know yourself," Ari responded.

"You thought," Samantha replied as she pulled down her sun visor.

She opened the mirror and adjusted her hair and Ari turned up the radio.

"And now, we have the latest from King Pin. This one is called 'Karma' by Lester the Prophet featuring Ari Love," the radio personality announced. *"King Pin has been relatively silent since the attack from T.K. Nation and Kai-G's first and only reply, but it's good to see they're rising above and are pushing forward. Check it out."*

The instrumental started and Ari started to rap along with Lester.

"Killer vibes for killer minds, man that shit is incredible
I bought you rings, I bought you shoes, man I felt you were worth it, yo
This money that I'm countin', it's steady bringin' me joy
But I'm not lettin' it define me, man that ish is unethical
Baby girl, it makes no sense you wanna see me in federal
For ish I did for you, don't you see that it's critical
This my life, this my glory, it's all in your hands
And you would rather see me fail than to see this paper fold
But when this ish hits the streets, hits the net, and the radio
Don't you come runnin' back to me like some kind of –
Wait

Don't mean disrespect
But if you're coming for me, you better make sure you come
correct
These are the seeds I'm planting, and I'm telling you that this ish
is not joke
You got me paralyzed, waist down
Man, I sometimes choke
I'm settin' the vision and believe it's gon' work
And baby, if you can't get with that, you gon have to watch and
learn.
Let's go."

"Let me find out that Ari has a flow to her," Samantha chuckled.
"I dabble a little bit," Ari laughed. "But I'm not a rapper though,"
she smirked.
Samantha playfully hit her in the shoulder.
"You and Lester got a hit," Samantha added as Ari turned into the
parking lot.
"Here comes my favorite part," Ari laughed as her verse in the
song came on.

" *Time waits for no one, this you should know*
I'm that 'b' from the streets, and I got this mean flow
(No period, haha)
You toyed with me boy," she sang, *"this ish is no joke*
My heart is not a toy that you can leave on the floor
One of these days, this is gonna come back and you gon' see
Your love for Ari Love is the only thing keepin' you with Bri
What you see in her, you used to see in me
But karma's coming around and you know that's a real b.
I'm gonna sit back and watch
I'll love you from afar
But I can't act like you're the only thing that matters
Playa, understand I'm gonna go far
I'm gonna reach new heights and tell the world
A-R-I, you better watch out for this girl."

Ari put the car in park and a smirk appeared on her face.
Samantha chuckled at Ari and clapped her hands; Kailyn did the same.

"You got a little something, girl," Samantha uttered.

"More like a lot of something," Ari boasted.

"Don't get cocky, now," Samantha joked as she opened the car door.

"Give me a reason not to be," Ari exited the vehicle and opened the back door.

Kailyn unbuckled her seat belt and scooted to the door.
Ari reached her arms out and helped Kailyn out of the vehicle.

"You're getting big," she spoke as Kailyn's feet connected to the Earth.

She kissed Kailyn on the cheek and stood erect.

"Girl, don't hurt your back lifting that girl," Samantha chuckled.
Ari laughed and they both walked to the entrance of the mall.

A man ran up with a camera and took pictures of the three of them.

"Samantha, Ari: over here!" he called out while taking the pictures.

Samantha did her best to shield Kailyn from the cameraman.
Samantha picked Kailyn up and walked alongside Ari.

"Sam, stay close," Ari directed as she held Samantha's free hand.
The cameraman stayed directly in their faces taking pictures.
Ari knew not to say or do anything that could jeopardize her career or the group's reputation.

"Get out of here," she spoke as she and Samantha ran into the bathroom once they entered the mall.

"What can you tell us about Lester's new album?" the man yelled through the door.

Ari sighed.

"We should be good for now," she uttered. "God, I don't know why these paparazzi don't take 'no' for an answer."

Samantha thought.

"Where are the security guards that Kaiden hired?" she asked.

"I came out on my own," Ari admitted. "I didn't bring any security. Didn't think I would need it."

Samantha laughed.

"Girl, you are on top of the charts right now, not to mention you are bad a-f," she didn't want to curse in front of Kailyn. "You got all the men flockin'; you definitely need security."

Ari grinned.

"I mean, I don't like to brag, but..." she threw her hair.

"You are something else," Samantha smirked and looked in the bathroom mirror. "So, what? We're supposed to camp out in this bathroom all day?"

"No," Ari laughed. "I'll just call some of the security guards to come and escort us if we're going to have to be dealing with the cameras and crap."

"Better call them, girl. Because if something happens to us that could be prevented," Samantha breathed through her nose and groaned.

"We'll be fine. Just relax," Ari giggled.

Ari pulled out her phone and dialed a number.

While Ari was talking, Samantha sat Kailyn on the sink. She then checked her phone for a potential message from Kaiden.

There were no messages from him, and he hadn't been active on social media for the past few hours.

"They're in the area," Ari spoke as she hung up her phone. "A few guards should be over here in the next five minutes."

"Where's Smoove?" Samantha questioned.

"Probably running around somewhere looking for food," Ari laughed. "That boy is always in someone's refrigerator."

Samantha chuckled at the comment.

"At least you got tabs on him," she spoke.

"Sam don't worry about Kaiden," Ari spoke. "As much as you're thinking about him, I guarantee you that he is thinking about you."

"Interestingly enough, Mama Green said the same thing," Samantha thought aloud.

"So, there must be some truth to it," Ari continued. "I may be Kaiden's artist, but I'm also like a sister to him. The man can't get enough of talking about you," she finished.

Samantha smiled slightly and touched Kailyn's hair.

There was a knock at the door before a gruff voice spoke.

"Ms. Love, it's Dennis."

Ari sighed a small sigh of relief.

"Come on, girl," she spoke to Samantha. "That's the security guard."

Samantha held Kailyn's hand and they all walked out of the bathroom.

"Stay low and stay close," Dennis spoke.

Dennis stood at 6'7, which towered over the two ladies.

"That won't be hard to do," Samantha joked.

"Nice to see you, Mrs. Green," Dennis chuckled. "I've brought along Alonzo Wesley, Gregory Hardin, and James Fullett," he continued to speak.

The three were around the same height as Dennis and simultaneously nodded their heads.

"We will be in the diamond formation: meaning our movements and lineup will resemble the geometric configuration of a diamond, with a guard covering each corner. Mrs. Green, Ms. Love, and Ms. Green," he referred to Kailyn, "will be in the center of the diamond."

Samantha and Ari looked at each other.

"The idea is to give you 360 degrees of protection," James added.

"It is vital that we stay tightly packed in formation. Your safety is our primary concern," Alonzo continued.

"Let us know of the stores you all will be visiting and the order so that we can best protect you," Gregory spoke. "While in the store, we will loosen the formation so you can shop, but we will tighten the formation as needed."

"If any paparazzi approach, we will tighten the formation so that no unwanted photography is obtained. If someone tries to attack or harm you all in any way, we will be required to use deadly force, if needed, to keep you safe."

The men all raised their shirts slightly and revealed holsters with guns in them.

"We are all licensed to carry," Dennis added. "The objective is that everyone goes home safely, and you all are well protected. We have a job to do, and by hook or crook, we're going to get it done."

"Do you all understand the formation presented and what steps we will be taking to ensure your safety?"

"Understood," Ari replied.

The six of them entered the formation and Ari called out the first store they were going to.

"This should be easy," Samantha laughed as the men escorted them through the store.

"Yeah, girl," Ari laughed.

"Mommy, who are they?" Kailyn asked inquisitively.

"They're here to keep us safe," Samantha answered.

"But why? Doesn't *Daa-yee* keep us safe?" she innocently continued.

Samantha swallowed air.

"He does," she began, "but Daddy is busy right now," she spoke softly to Kailyn.

Ari put her hand on Samantha's shoulder.

"So, since he isn't here, these men are here for our protection."

"Why do we need pro, pro, *proteshion*?" she struggled to say the word.

"It's because Mommy and Daddy are stars," Ari intervened. "And, a lot of people want what Mommy and Daddy have. You don't want them to take it, right?"

"No," Kailyn spoke as she shook her head.

Samantha chuckled at Ari's comment about her being a star.

"Now we all know that you're the true star, Ari," Samantha laughed. "I'm just the star's wife," she shrugged her shoulders.

Kailyn looked at her doll and hugged it.

Samantha looked back up at the guards.

"Diamond formation," Dennis called; the security guards moved in unison.

Samantha picked up Kailyn and stood in the middle as the guards packed tightly around the three of them.

"Land of the Free," Ari spoke.

"Land of the Free," Dennis repeated over his earpiece to the other three guards.

As the seven of them walked down the mall's hallway, shoppers were trying to get a glimpse of who the men were guarding; many of the shoppers tried to get closer and the guards often closed in around Samantha, Ari, and Kailyn to obstruct the view.

"Damn," Samantha uttered. "Are things always this closely guarded?" Samantha asked.

"Not always this heavy," Ari replied, "but these men don't play. They are not only guarding one of *King Pin*'s artists, but they are guarding the leader. Kaiden has told them the role of everyone in K.P.; you and Kailyn are at the top of the assets list; even higher than him. Not to mention, they take security *very* seriously."

"This is too much," Samantha chuckled. "Men, stand down," Samantha spoke.

The guards stopped walking but never broke formation.

"Mrs. Green, we don't think that's wise," Alonzo replied.

"We want security; not baby sitters," Samantha stated with a slight laugh, yet she was serious. "You all can trail behind Ari and me," she instructed as she held Kailyn. "Right now, we're in a public place and the threat level is low aside from paparazzi, so we don't need to be led and heavily guarded. Save that for when we go outside."

"Mrs. Green," Gregory started.

"Let's not forget that I'm the one who will sign your checks," Samantha spoke sternly. "Stand down."

Dennis slightly shook his head but surrendered.

"Calling an audible," he spoke over his earpiece. "Football formation: Shotgun Max Protect," he called.

The guards quickly realigned so that the four of them stood side-by-side behind Ari and Samantha.

"Thank you," Samantha spoke.

Shoppers were stoked to see Ari, and many tried to run over for a picture with her.

"Diamond formation, tight," Dennis spoke over the earpiece as the fans quickly approached.

The guards quickly changed their formation to protect Samantha, Ari, and Kailyn.

The fans stopped rushing as the bodyguards blocked access to the trio.

"We're allowing pictures with fans, just not having interviews and things with paparazzi," Samantha spoke aloud. "We can't dissolve the relationship we have them."

"Please note that this is not the intention, Mrs. Green," Dennis spoke, never looking away from the crowd. "We'll control the situation," he nodded slightly.

"Ladies and gentlemen," Dennis spoke to the crowd, "if you all want pictures with Mrs. Green or Ari Love, we will have order, or else there won't be any allowed."

Alonzo, Gregory, and James stayed around Ari, Kailyn, and Samantha as Dennis spoke.

The fans were excited and chatting loudly as Dennis spoke over the earpiece.

"Protect the package."

***

Ari and Samantha rose from the chairs in the food court and the security guards stood in unison.

"All finished?" Alonzo asked.

"Yes," Ari spoke. "Just going back to the car and then we're good to go."

Samantha opened the binder in her hand and took out four checks that she'd written for the guards.

"Yes mam," Dennis spoke. "Diamond formation, tight" he spoke aloud.

Alonzo, Gregory, and James quickly lined up in the appropriate formation. "Once we get to the vehicle, we will break formation, but keep the packages covered. Wesley and Hardin, you will cover Ms. Love while she enters the vehicle; I and Fullet will protect Mrs. Green and Ms. Green as they enter. Once the clients are fully engaged in their vehicle, Hardin and Fullett will then separate and retrieve the security trucks," Dennis explained and cleared his throat.

Samantha paid close attention to what the final plan was.

"Once Hardin and Fullet arrive back to the client vehicle with the security cars, we will escort the ladies out of the parking lot and to their destination."

"We won't need security past the parking lot," Samantha interjected. "Where we're headed, we don't want people to know our status, so we're keeping a low profile."

"As you wish," Dennis spoke. "Once we leave the parking lot, guards will regroup at *Home Station*," he corrected. "Mrs. Green, Ms. Love: we are at your service 25/8, so please don't hesitate to call us when needed," he finished.

"Mommy, where's *Daa-yee*?" Kailyn asked as she tugged at Samantha's shirt.

"I'm not sure, baby," Samantha spoke. "When we get to the car, you can call him, okay?"

"Okay, Mommy."

"On your move," Dennis spoke to Samantha.
Samantha took the first step and all the men moved in unison.
"Keep it tight," Dennis spoke over the earpiece and they all exited the mall.
The sun shined brightly and the seven of them walked to the vehicle.
"Watch your six and nine," Dennis spoke gruffly.
Alonzo and Gregory tightened their sides of the formation; closing the gap between them and the ladies.
As they all arrived at the car, Alonzo and Gregory stayed on the driver's side to protect Ari, while Dennis and James walked to the opposing side with Samantha and Kailyn.
Samantha buckled Kailyn in the backseat before turning around and giving the checks to Dennis.
"Thank you," she spoke as she got inside of the car.
Dennis closed the door behind her.
"It is our pleasure to serve you," he uttered.
Ari started the car; James and Gregory walked away to retrieve the security cars.
She lowered her voice to a whisper.

"How much did you give them?" she asked Samantha.
Samantha chuckled.
"I gave Dennis 750, and the rest got 500. Why, what's up?"
"Damn girl," she laughed. "Kaiden normally only gives them 350 a pop and 500 to the leader."
"Oh well," Samantha laughed, "let them live a little. *King Pin* can afford it."

Samantha dialed Kaiden's phone number and gave Kailyn her phone.
Kailyn tapped the speaker icon and Kaiden answered.

"Hello," he answered.

"Hey *Daa-yee*," Kailyn spoke enthusiastically.

"Hey baby girl," Kaiden replied. "How are you doing?"

"I'm fine," she answered. "Where are you?" she asked.

"Daddy's sitting here with Byron in the studio," he answered.

"And, where are you?"

"At the mall," she replied instantly.

"Who's with you?" Kaiden questioned.

"Mommy and *Ah-wee*," Kailyn spoke. "*Daa-yee*, I miss you," Kailyn added.

"Daddy misses you all too."

Samantha's heart fluttered hearing Kaiden's voice and hearing him say how he missed them.

7

"Don't make my girl suffer for what I did, Kai," Christina spoke to Kaiden over the phone.

Kaiden continued to edit the track he'd been producing for Lester's album.

"It's been almost a month," Christina uttered. "And you know she wouldn't do anything to hurt you."

Kaiden's ego wouldn't let him back down or for his anger to subside.

"I don't know what's real anymore," Kaiden shook his head as he ensured that Lester's vocals lined up with the instrumental.

Christina sighed and continued.

"What are you doing?" she asked.

"Just working," Kaiden responded. "Finishing this track for Lester's album so that we can set a release date."

"This is his debut album, correct?"

"It is," Kaiden spoke. "We've been working hard to make it happen," he slightly smiled at his accomplishment.

"I'm about to come over," Christina directed.

"Knock yourself out," he laughed. "I could use the company."

"Bet," she spoke. "Be there soon."

Kaiden ended the call and pressed play on the track.
"Man of the streets, man of the town, man of the house
Devouring the tracks and digesting the shits, faster than you can
count
Makin' these moves and stacking this paper, makin' sure this shit
drops
When this shit hits the net, you're gonna see my name pop."

Kaiden moved the verse and repositioned it in the song.
"Just gotta make him adlib a bit and I think it'll be good," Kaiden
pressed save.
He sent a text to Lester.

Kaiden: Prophet, let's get you in the studio at some point to put
the final touches on your project

Lester replied seconds later.

Prophet: Okay, cool. I got you

Kaiden put his phone in his pocket and the doorbell rang.
He looked at the camera and saw Christina standing there; she
was alone.
"I'm in the studio, Tina. Come on in," Kaiden pressed the button
and unlocked the door.
Christina entered the home and walked down to the studio.
"What's up Tina?" Kaiden asked as she walked down the stairs.
"Nothing," she replied. "I'm loving what you've done to the
studio," she noticed the remodeling he'd done.
"It's nothing major," Kaiden shrugged his shoulders. "It had to be
done, though."
He closed the track he was working on for Lester.
"You heard from Samantha?" he asked.
"Not today," Christina answered as she sat in the chair next to
Kaiden. "She was all good yesterday though."

"She's at my mom's," Kaiden spoke. "So, I know she and Kailyn are well taken care of. How's Isaias?" he asked.

"He's well," Christina spoke as she rose to her feet. "Kai, I never really thanked you for saving my boy's life," she smiled.

"Nah, it's no need to thank me, Tina. You know that's my little guy," Kaiden chuckled.

"I don't think you understand how much that meant to me. You risked your life to save Isaias and Kailyn, and that speaks volumes about your character."

"Yeah, so why is it so hard to understand that I'm all in?" he referred to his argument with Samantha.

Christina took a deep breath.

"Kaiden, I hurt you. I understand that, but that's not who Samantha is," Christina defended her friend.

Kaiden side-eyed Christina.

"I'm telling you the truth," she replied. "Samantha wouldn't ever do anything to hurt you." Christina shook her head and continued. "She's not dumb like me. So, the shit that Eddy is saying, you have to understand that he's lying."

Christina paced the floor.

"Look, Kai," she continued, "you can hate me and be mad at me forever because of what happened, but don't take it out on her. She truly loves you," Christina uttered. "You may resent me until the end of time. You may never ever trust me again, and that's my fuck up. You may be cautious with your heart, but that's on me. I broke you, Kai, but Samantha has fixed you... and she wouldn't fix you just to break you down," Christina finished.

Kaiden thought about what Christina had said.

"I did what I did because I wasn't wise enough to see what the hell I had in front of me. I wanted to have my cake and to eat it too," Christina slightly teared up.

"Jordan was my boy toy," she added, "but I realized that he wasn't what I wanted or needed in my life; it was you all along."

She straightened her composure.

"I'm not telling you this because I want to be with you, Kai. I'm telling you this for closure," Christina assured him. "Don't take your anger at me out on Sam."

Kaiden lightly sighed.

"The way I acted with Sammy, I don't think she'd even be willing to forgive me," Kaiden chuckled with disgust.

"Kai, she loves you," Christina stated again. "She's already forgiven you.

Way before she had to," she slightly shrugged her shoulders.

"How can you be so sure?" Kaiden questioned.

"When Samantha speaks to me, it's all about you. How you would treat her and Kailyn; the little faces you make when you're in the studio producing music with your artists; the way you put her first; the way you play with Kailyn," Christina rolled her eyes and laughed. "Kaiden, you are Samantha's world."

It warmed Kaiden's heart to hear this, and he felt terrible about how he'd acted with her.

"Here," Christina spoke, and she reached her arms out for an embrace.

Kaiden hugged Christina tightly and let out a tear.

No words were spoken during their embrace, but it seemed as though they were both thinking the same thing.

"Kai, you've been a blessing to both Samantha and me. And I know you've been more than a blessing to Isaias and Kailyn. Be the man that I know you are," Christina spoke softly and passed him his phone from the mixer. "Call her."

She kissed him on the cheek and returned to her seat.

He unlocked his phone and went to his text messages. He saw Samantha's name at the top and opened it.

"You can't do it, huh?" Christina asked as she noticed his hesitation.

"I was such an ass to her," he chuckled. "I don't even know where to start."

"Well, you know where she is," Christina responded. "Go to her."

▪▪

"Hello?" Kaiden answered his phone as he left the store.

"You ready to give me half of *my* company?" Eddy questioned.

"Not today, man," Kaiden replied as he unlocked his car door.

"Kaiden, I'm not playing with you, nigga. I want what's mine and I'm going to do whatever needs to be done to get it."

"Shit, bro," Kaiden started as he entered his vehicle, "you can keep the threats coming, but I'm not concerned." Kaiden adjusted his rearview mirror. "You want *King Pin*, you're going to have to come take it from me, straight up," Kaiden fiercely added.

Eddy chuckled.

"Bet. Keep your eyes on your business," he spoke. "Kailyn, Samantha, Ari, Byron, Lester, *King Pin*; all of it."

"What did I tell you before?" Kaiden asked. "Keep them out of your mouth and we won't have a problem."

"Hold up, I think I see Samantha now," Eddy hung up his phone. Kaiden paid no mind to his comment and began his drive to his mother's home.

Kaiden merged on the expressway and merged into traffic. His phone rang and he answered it.

"What's good, Ma?" he answered the phone.

"Kai, I don't know what's going on or where you are, but you need to get over here," his mother spoke over the phone.

"I'm on my way there now, but what's going on?" Kaiden asked.

"Edward is over here and is outside playing with Kailyn right now. Samantha is telling him to go away, but his advancements towards her are concerning. I even went out there, but he doesn't seem to care," she spoke and walked to the window. "I think he may be on drugs," she suggested.

Anger quickly built inside of Kaiden and he accelerated.

"This bitch," he whispered. "Ma, I'm on my way. I'll be there soon." Kaiden hung up the phone and opened his glove compartment.

His concealed-carry card fell to the front of the compartment and Kaiden removed all the papers with his free hand and opened the additional compartment.
He pulled out a black handgun and placed it under the seat. He returned the papers and closed the compartment with his free hand.
He continued to speed and switched lanes; he was determined to cut this hour-long drive down to 30 minutes.

"This nigga has a death wish," Kaiden chuckled to himself. "I know damn well he isn't over my mom's crib fucking with my wife and child."
He picked up his phone and dialed Ari.
"Hello?" she answered.
"What's good Ari? It's Kai," he assumed she was with Byron. "You with Smoove?"
Although the two of them hadn't said anything, Kaiden knew they were dating.
"Hey Kai. Yeah, he's right here," she replied. "You wanna talk to him."
"Nah, it's cool," Kaiden spoke. "Where y'all at? Y'all close to my mom's?"
"We're in the area," Ari responded. "Maybe about ten minutes away from there. What's up?" Ari was concerned at the tone of his voice and put Kaiden on speakerphone.
"Eddy is at my mom's crib," Kaiden spoke with anger as he drove. "He's there with Samantha and Kailyn. I'm on my way but I need for you to swing by there since you're closer, and hold his ass there," Kaiden authorized.

"We got you, bro," Byron spoke over the phone.
"I'll be there in about 30."
Kaiden hung up the phone and continued to drive.

"This nigga thinks I'm playing with him."
***
Kaiden arrived at his mother's home and saw Byron's car parked in front.

He tucked the gun under his belt and exited the vehicle, slamming the car door behind him.

Kaiden walked through the gate and called out Samantha's name.

"*Daa-yee*!" Kailyn shouted and ran to him for an embrace.

"Hey, baby girl," he spoke.

Kaiden was careful as he hugged Kailyn, as he knew she was level to the firearm.

"Where's Mommy?" Kaiden asked.

"She's back there with Uncle Eddy," Kailyn replied innocently. "She's mad at him. *Ah-wee* and By are here."

Kaiden knew she had trouble pronouncing 'Byron', so she shortened it to By.

"You don't have to call Eddy that, he's not your uncle anymore," Kaiden started. "Baby girl, do me a favor. Go in the house with Grandma for a bit," Kaiden kissed her on the forehead and Kailyn walked into the home.

He pulled out the weapon and continued to march into the backyard.

"You thought I was fucking playing?" Kaiden asked as he entered the yard, aiming the weapon at Eddy.

Kaiden saw Ari and Byron near him; Ari was speaking to Samantha in a low tone and Byron was nearly shouting at Eddy.

All seemed to cease once they saw Kaiden and the weapon.

Eddy was holding Samantha's arms as she tried to pull away. She felt a warmth overcome her as she saw Kaiden.

"Let her go, now!" Kaiden demanded.

Eddy chuckled.

"You ready to give me half my shit?" Eddy spoke.

"I'll give your ass half a bullet," Kaiden warned. "As I told you over the phone, you're gonna have to take it from me straight up."
"Don't worry about me. I'm gonna get my shit one way or the other," Eddy spoke.
"Me too," Kaiden spoke as he cocked the gun.

"Good ol' Kai-G," he released Samantha's grip. "A nigga got tough ever since his bitch ass got shot on tour." Eddy looked at the weapon. "Look at you, now. You come back here with a damn gun. Aren't you the same muthafucka that preaches that we need to stop killing each other?"
"I've given your ass enough warnings to stay away from my family. You want a rap beef, we do this shit in the music," Kaiden protected as he motioned for Samantha to come to him. "But if you want bloody," he gritted his teeth, "we can do that, too."
Samantha walked over to him.
"So, you're gonna kill me over this beef?"
Kaiden positioned his finger on the trigger.

"Baby, don't do it," Samantha spoke to him. "Kailyn and I are fine."
"Boss, give me the gun," Byron inched closer to Kaiden with his hand extended.
Kaiden bit his lip and glared at Eddy.
"I shoot you and I'm going straight to a cell," Kaiden scoffed. "I got a family that needs me and means more to me than this bullshit."
Eddy laughed.
"Nigga, you don't have shit. This right here," he pointed to Samantha, "that ass is for everybody. Like I said, you need to go and get checked to see if Kailyn is yours."
"You a *buford*," Kaiden spoke. "A goofy ass nigga. You need to chill with that shit before I make this gun sing," Kaiden threatened.
"It seems like I struck a nerve," Eddy chuckled. "Don't worry. Everything that happens in the dark *always* comes to light. Right?"

Kaiden slightly shook his head.

"Keep talkin' that shit and I'll put a hot one in you," he asserted.
"Kai, calm down," Samantha pleaded.
"You are so fuckin' lucky," Kaiden chuckled. "Get the fuck out of my mom's yard," he threatened. "And if you come near Samantha or Kailyn again, I'm on yo' ass," Kaiden spoke.
"It's rap beef," Eddy replied. "I guess you wanna be the next Pac or B.I.G.," Eddy laughed.
Kaiden lowered the gun and passed it to Byron.

"It doesn't even need to escalate like that," Kaiden replied. "But stay the fuck away from my family."
"Why the fuck is she over here without you anyway?" Eddy shouted. "I guess you do believe what I was saying," he chuckled.
Kaiden wondered how he knew that Samantha was there.

"Keep playin' with me, Eddy," Kaiden responded.
Eddy walked past and brushed his hand against Samantha's.
She jerked her hand back.
"Damn, you still fine," Eddy smirked.
Kaiden turned and punched Eddy in the face as soon as he made the remark.
"Boss!" Byron exclaimed as he quickly dropped the gun and grabbed Kaiden.
Eddy grabbed his face and felt blood trickling from his nose.
"Man, what the fuck?" Eddy asserted.
"Eddy, just leave," Ari spoke.
Eddy looked at Byron and Ari while holding his nose.
"The two love birds," he laughed. "Sticking together as always; I see ya'," he laughed before leaving the yard.

Byron picked up the firearm and unloaded the weapon. He removed the bullet from the chamber.
Kaiden turned and faced Samantha. He quickly embraced her.

"I'm sorry, babe," he spoke as he stroked her hair.
He followed the apology with a kiss on the lips.

Samantha let out a tear and slapped Kaiden.

"Don't you ever do no dumb shit like that again," she chuckled and was teary-eyed. "You get locked away in a cell or end up in a box, I will lose my fucking mind."

She hugged him tightly.

"I love you."

Kaiden smirked although there was a slight tingle in his face.

"That's my baby," he kissed her forehead.

Byron and Ari walked closer.

"Damn, so what's next?" Ari asked.

"Yeah, man," Byron spoke. "This shit has escalated."

"Stay on your toes," Kaiden spoke with authority as he held Samantha; he was disappointed that it had come to this. "I already know that Eddy isn't going to take me pulling a gun on him lightly."

"Say the word," Byron spoke. "*King Pin* is ready for it," he chuckled and handed Kaiden the gun.

"No smoke," Kaiden chuckled. "He just took me out of my element for a moment when he came over and decided to mess with my family," he admitted. "I don't care about the rap beef; I'll leave that to the music and hopefully he does the same."

Kaiden's mom stepped out of the home with Kailyn.

Kaiden quickly put the gun away.

"What's going on?" Mama Green asked.

"Everything's cool," Kaiden spoke. "I don't think he'll be back over here unless he's invited," he examined his knuckles.

Kailyn ran over to Kaiden and he picked her up.

"Let's go home," he kissed Samantha on the lips once more.

8

Months passed since the incident between Kaiden and Eddy, and all had been silent in terms of the rap beef.
The team thought of an idea that was sure to make noise over the release of Lester's album.

"This is how we're going to do this," Kaiden spoke as the team and Christina sat in the studio.
Samantha had taken Isaias and Kailyn to the store with her to do some shopping for the upcoming event.
"Lester, you're going to do radio interviews. If they come for you, I want you to be on top of them."
"I got you," Lester nodded in agreement.

"Ari and Smoove, take advantage of the *Bari* gang," he announced.
Ari and Byron looked at each other and displayed a confused look towards Kaiden.
"We all know," Kaiden chuckled. "I'm fine with it as long as it doesn't interfere with our work," Kaiden referred to their relationship.
The two let out a small sigh and laughed.
"We got you," Byron spoke.

"Let's make this an exclusive event, where the fans are damn near breaking down the door to get in," Kaiden spoke with excitement. "And we have the power to make that happen," Ari replied. "We all just have to put in the work to do so."

There was a knock at the door, and they all looked at each other. "How convenient is it that I disabled the live view of the cameras for maintenance?" Kaiden chuckled. He rose to his feet. "Y'all keep brainstorming," he smiled, "I'll be back."
"I'll come with you," Christina rose from the chair and walked behind Kaiden up the stairs.
"You know I'm a big boy, right?" Kaiden laughed.
"We all need security," Christina grinned.
"Not to be rude, but what would *you* do if something were to pop off?" he jokingly asked.
She laughed and playfully hit him in the shoulder.
"Shut up, stupid."
Kaiden put his arm around her shoulder.
"Nah, but for real, I'm a protector. The way I protected Isaias and Kailyn from the bullets, I'll do the same thing again if needed."

Christina looked at Kaiden dreamily.
This was the man she fell in love with, but she couldn't show her emotions.
Kaiden was married to her best friend, and she was in a happy relationship with Trequan.
The two arrived at the door and Kaiden opened it.

"Kaiden Green!" Eddy exclaimed.
Kaiden scoffed at Eddy.
"I brought my own paparazzi," he laughed.
Kaiden saw that Eddy was under the influence of something.
Kaiden observed the members of *T.K. Nation* in his yard.

"Hey Kai," Jada called as she had her hand on his car.

Christina looked at Kaiden; he remained calm even though this was occurring.

Kaiden clapped his hands together slowly.

"I must say I'm surprised," he chuckled. "You were able to bring everyone together who sees me as a threat, when the focus is on the wrong individual," he slightly shrugged his shoulders.

Eddy eyed Kaiden up and down.

"This is your threat," Kaiden referenced Eddy to the group. "He's consistently getting drunk and high; how in the hell do you expect your careers to grow?"

Jada, Damien, and Bishop all looked at each other as if they agreed with what Kaiden was saying.

"This is why he's no longer part of *King Pin*," he finished. "It's this shit right here."

Christina held Kaiden's arm to keep him peaceful.

"Shut up, bitch," Eddy spoke, and he got closer to Kaiden's face.

Eddy laughed lightly and continued.

"I give you a reason to be scared," he smirked. "*T.K. Nation* is quickly taking the world by storm and *King Pin* has no choice but to watch."

Kaiden didn't get upset by what Eddy was saying. Instead, he chuckled at his ex-friend and his behavior.

"Let's look at the numbers," Kaiden spoke gently. "Then we'll really see who's on top."

Eddy stared at Kaiden and chuckled before shaking his head.

"*T.K.* Nation, it's time for a revolution," he announced to his team. "Now is the time that we rise above and take control of this empire," Eddy announced to his team. "Fuck *King Pin*," he shouted.

"Eddy look at you: making a damn fool out of yourself," Christina spoke.

"But stacking this paper while doing it," he laughed.

Byron, Ari, and Lester came to the door and stood behind Kaiden. "Speaking of *King Pin*," he shouted, "welcome to the party Ari, Smoove, and Prophet."

Jada slowly approached and touched Eddy's shoulder.

"Come on, Boss. This wasn't the plan," she spoke softly.

"Jada, back up," Eddy spoke as he redirected his attention to Kaiden. "Let this be your warning shot, Kaiden Green. I don't play about mine."

"Keep it in the music," Kaiden calmly spoke. "Let your work speak for you."

"Boss, let's go," Jada repeated.

"Again, back the fuck up," Eddy spoke.

Kaiden looked at Jada and chuckled.

"And this is the guy that's supposed to lead you to victory and success?" Kaiden shook his head.

"Eddy, get away from my door."

"You want to play?" Eddy asked. "Watch me win."

Jada shook her head and spoke.

"Come on, Eddy," she spoke. "We don't need this kind of heat," she looked around as neighbors started to record on their phones.

" *T.K.* Nation, we out," Eddy spoke as he walked from the porch to his vehicle.

Bishop got into the vehicle with Eddy, and Jada and Damien rode together. They sped away from the home and Kaiden closed the door.

"Does he ever stop?" Ari chuckled.

"He realizes you can end his whole career, right?" Byron asked.

"And that's what he's afraid of," Kaiden spoke to his crew.

"Let him be scared," Lester shrugged his shoulders. "K.P., we've got work to do," he refocused everyone's attention, "so let's get back in the studio and finish brainstorming."

∎∎

"Congratulations, you're pregnant," the doctor spoke.

Samantha was ecstatic to hear the news; Christina, on the other hand, was speechless.

"How far along?" Samantha asked.

"About 12 weeks," the doctor replied. "Your small frame hides the pregnancy very well," he finished.

Samantha looked at her friend and hugged her as she sat on the examination table.

"Is it your first child?" she asked.

"No," Christina replied. "I have a son; he's six."

"Well, make sure you let him know that he's about to be a big brother," the doctor removed her gloves and washed her hands.

Samantha smiled at Christina and Christina forced a smile.

"I'll be back shortly with your follow-up paperwork and to address any concerns or questions you may have," the doctor spoke before leaving the room.

"Girl, you don't seem thrilled at all," Samantha chuckled.

"I am, but girl, what am I going to do with another child?" Christina asked.

"Be a great mother," Samantha chuckled.

Christina rolled her eyes at Samantha.

"I'm serious, girl."

Samantha studied her friend before speaking.

"He doesn't want children right now, does he?" she asked.

Christina looked at Samantha and spoke.

"Girl, I don't know what he wants," she admitted. "One day, he's all for it, the next moment, he's not."

"You have to tell him," Samantha spoke gently. "He deserves to know what's going on."

Christina was shaken up to know that she was pregnant. Part of this was because she didn't know how Trequan would take it, but another part of her was a little upset that she wasn't pregnant with Kaiden's child.

Although they hadn't been together for years, he was one of the only people she could envision having a child with.
She didn't dare tell Samantha the second part.

"I know," Christina uttered.
Samantha sat on the examination table beside Christina and embraced her friend.
"It's going to be okay," she spoke softly as the two hugged.
The doctor re-entered the room with a form.
"Okay, Ms. Parker, here's your follow-up date. I want to see you back here in exactly 4 weeks. Here's your prescription as well; take these for the headaches you've been experiencing."
"Thanks, Doctor Upton," Christina took the papers from the doctor and shook her hand.
"Do you all have any questions for me?" Doctor Upton asked.
"None right now," Christina replied. "But if something changes, I'll let you know."
"Thanks, Doc," Samantha spoke as she and Christina rose to their feet.
They grabbed their coats and left the office.

Chills ran down Christina's spine as she walked down the corridor of the building.
Samantha put her hand on Christina's shoulder as they walked; Christina felt as though everything was moving in slow motion.
Thoughts of Kaiden making love to her flashed through Christina's mind, although it wasn't necessarily Kaiden in her visions; the mannerisms belonged to Kaiden, but the actions and behavior belonged to Trequan. Her brain found a way to conjoin the two men.
As the two arrived at Samantha's car, Samantha got in the driver's seat while Christina got in the passenger chair.
Samantha started the vehicle and put on her seatbelt. Christina secured her seatbelt and Samantha reversed from the parking spot.

"It'll be okay, girl," she assured Christina.

"I hope so," Christina spoke.

Samantha continued the drive home; Christina looked out of the window and drew figures on the window with her finger.

Once they pulled into the driveway, the two sat in silence. Christina wondered if she should tell Samantha her thoughts about the pregnancy.

"You know you have to tell him," Samantha finally spoke.

"Who?" Christina asked.

"Who else?" Samantha nervously chuckled. "Trequan."

Samantha was suspicious of Christina's question.

"Who did you think I was talking about?"

Christina looked around for an exit.

"Answer me, girl," Samantha insisted.

Christina sighed.

"I thought you were talking about Kaiden, to be honest," Christina replied.

"Why would I be talking about Kaiden?" Samantha asked. "Unless there's something that I should know."

Christina could see the suspicion with Samantha. Part of her wanted to tell Samantha the truth, but the other half of her told her not to let Samantha know her thoughts.

"No, there's nothing to discuss with that. I just thought you were talking about him," she partially lied.

Samantha studied her friend.

"Uh-huh," she spoke before opening her door.

She closed the door and walked to the door. She opened the home and walked inside.

"Kai, we're back," she called.

She heard tiny footsteps approaching and she put her purse down.

Kailyn poked her head from around the corner and ran to her mother.

"Mommy!"

"Kai-kai," she squealed as she picked up the child. "Why hasn't your daddy done something to this head of yours?" she ran her fingers through Kailyn's hair.

Kailyn laughed.

"*Daa-yee* and Lester are downstairs. Lester's rapping," she replied.

"Does Daddy know where *you* are?" she asked Kailyn.

"He saw you on the screen and told me to come to you," she innocently spoke.

Samantha knew she had to ask Kaiden about what Christina had mentioned, but she didn't want to do it while he was conducting business.

"Oh, okay baby," she set Kailyn down. "Well tell Daddy that he needs to come see me himself," she kissed her daughter on the cheek.

"Okay, Mommy," Kailyn spoke before skipping to the stairs.

"And stop running, babe. You're gonna hurt yourself."

Kailyn obeyed and walked down the stairs.

Christina entered the home and closed the door behind her.

She knew Samantha was suspicious and upset at this point, so she was very careful with how she chose her words.

"What's for dinner?" she asked.

"Kailyn, Kaiden, and I may be having pizza," Samantha spoke. "I don't feel like cooking," she admitted.

"And what about me?" Christina chuckled.

"Call Tre and ask him what he's cooking," Samantha replied with a laugh as she pulled the wine from the cabinet.

She poured herself a glass and sipped it before continuing.

"I would offer you some, girl, but you can't drink anything."

"Don't remind me," Christina uttered.

Kailyn entered the kitchen and stood next to her mom.

"Mommy, he said to come downstairs," she innocently spoke.

"Let's go see what this workaholic is up to," Samantha spoke as she sipped the wine.

She ran her hand through Kailyn's hair and Kailyn led the two down to the studio.

"*Daa-yee*, Mommy's here!" Kailyn spoke excitedly.

Kaiden looked up from the mixing board and saw Samantha.

"Hey, babe," he uttered, followed by a quick kiss on the lips. "Hey Tina," he spoke.

Samantha gave him a look of disapproval and didn't have to say more; Kaiden knew something was wrong.

"Hey Kai," Christina spoke as she went for a hug from Kaiden.

He gave her a hug and returned to the board.

"What y'all working on?" Samantha asked.

"Wrapping up the album," Kaiden replied. "The last track, actually," Kaiden looked at his notepad.

"What's the promotion strategy?" she asked.

"Hitting radio, hard," Kaiden admitted. "Interviews, his first single, etc. And we are going to put focus into getting this listening party poppin'," Kaiden spoke joyously.

He wanted to ask her about the budget they had available to allocate for Lester's album, but he knew to wait to ask for this information.

"Well, remember we have to plan accordingly," Samantha suggested.

He knew what she meant by this.

"Okay, babe."

The instrumental ended and Lester finished his rap.

"Alright, Prophet," Kaiden spoke over the microphone, "let's take five."

***

"Lester has been making a lot of noise," Ari suggested as she and Kaiden walked back to the car.

"I told you," he chuckled, "we just had to give him some time."

"You did," Ari admitted. "The important thing is that he's delivering now. Where are we with the listening party?" she asked.

"Well, after the promotion, Samantha says we still have about 10-k set aside for the event."

Ari thought for a moment and spoke.

"You wanna go through all of that for the event?" Ari asked.

"I'm thinking we go through a little more than half of it, at the very least," Kaiden unlocked the car door with the remote, "and either give the rest to him as a bonus or just put it away for later. I mean, it's his money anyway," Kaiden chuckled.

"That sounds like a plan to me," Ari replied.

As they arrived at the car, they were approached by three gentlemen.

"Kai-G? Ari Love?" one of the men spoke to Kaiden and Ari.

"That's us," Kaiden chuckled. "What y'all need, brother? An autograph?"

All the men removed their hats and they were all dressed in similar clothing.

"1... 2... 1-2-3," one of the men counted.

One of the gentlemen pulled out his phone and increased the volume. He pressed play, and music began to play from the Bluetooth speaker in his bag.

Kaiden waved his hand to Ari and she pulled out her phone to record the group. She walked to the side of Kaiden while recording the three.

The man who pulled out the phone and the silent one thus far began to harmonize the background vocals.

"*Hey, girl,*" the one who was silent finally spoke. "*I know we've been going through it lately. But I just want you to know that I love you and I would never ever do anything to hurt you.*"

"*Don't you cry, we'll get by, I won't tell you a lie, baby girl*
You gon' try, I'm gon' fight, we'll be fine, I will give you the world
Time's unkind, I won't lie, we gon' ride. Perfect; boy and a girl

Out of time, we gon' find, love is blind, time to watch it unfurl
Yesterday was the day, I won't play, I'm gon' tell you the truth
Rapidly, is the way, that you strayed, come on back to me, boo
If you stay, things will change, ándale, baby girl, here's the proof
Surprisingly, on one knee, marry me, baby, just say 'I do'.'"
Kaiden was a little surprised that the trio was approaching him
with a ballad, but he was intrigued by their approach and the
production of the instrumental; the lyrics and their voices weren't
bad either.

The man who approached Kaiden began to sing.
"Girl, I know that we've been through some things
But I don't want you to believe, no
That this wasn't meant to be
He strategically placed you with me
Baby, this is no mistake
Known each other since the 1st grade, whoo
But now it's time to pave the way
Give you this ring, marry me, girl, come make my day," the
approacher finished and stepped back.
As the approacher stepped back, one of the vocalizers took his
position.
"With you and me, it's destiny
Like two love birds sitting in the tree
Hoping you'd give me the key
A chance, at romance, girl come and get with me
I know we've been through some fights
And I'm not saying this shit is right, oh no
But baby girl, let's get this tight
And let me make you my wife," the man sang with passion and
soul.

He was about to continue his song when Kaiden held up a finger.
The three looked at him. Ari didn't show any emotion, although
she knew what Kaiden was thinking.
"Who are your inspirations?" Kaiden asked.

"Jagged Edge is a big one," the approacher spoke. "A lot of R&B groups from the 90s."

Kaiden and Ari nodded their heads.

"How old are you and what do you all call yourselves?" he asked.

"Well, I'm Francis King. I'm 23," the approacher spoke, "and these are my brothers: Emmanuel King, 21, and Zayne King, 18. We are *The Three Kingz*," the approacher spoke with confidence.

The instrumental continued to play in the background and Kaiden continued.

"Who made the beat?" he asked.

"I did, sir," Emmanuel spoke.

"You're the one that played it," Kaiden chuckled. "I guess you got a lot of pride in your work."

"And you must be Zayne," Ari spoke to the guy who was speaking at the beginning of the piece. "A-k-a the baritone of the group."

"A-k-a the baby of the group," Zayne chuckled.

Kaiden was silent.

"Mr. Green, we know you and Ms. Love are busy people, but we would like to get your feedback on our music," Francis spoke.

Kaiden looked at Ari before speaking.

"You all are very bold," Kaiden chuckled. "You all approach us and just start performing."

"You guys have confidence," Ari continued. "And that confidence is going to take you places."

Kaiden nodded in agreement.

The three gentlemen slightly lowered their heads.

"I understand," Francis spoke, disappointed.

"Why the long faces?" Kaiden asked.

The three looked up.

"It was hot," Kaiden chuckled. "It gave me a 90s vibe, just like your inspirations. But here," Kaiden passed Francis his card, "shoot me an email and we'll set up an appointment to get you all to come through and perform in front of *King Pin*," Kaiden chuckled and passed a card to Francis.

"Wait, for real?" Emmanuel asked.

Kaiden opened the door to the car and Ari walked around and opened hers.

"Who knows?" Ari chuckled. "Maybe we'll work on that song you all just performed," she smirked.

"Thank you all so much," Francis spoke.

"Do me two favors though," Kaiden spoke.

"Yeah?" Francis asked.

"One: get some steps in to go with your performance," Kaiden spoke.

"Working on choreography now," Zayne spoke.

"What's the other favor?" Emmanuel asked.

Kaiden smirked.

"Don't take a picture of my car and track me down," he laughed.

The gentlemen all laughed.

"I'll be looking for that email," Kaiden spoke before driving away.

Kaiden drove away and looked in his rearview mirror.

He saw the boys were ecstatic and giving each other hugs in awe of what just occurred.

"That was dope, Kai," Ari started. "K.P. has never worked with an R&B group before. It could make a lot of noise," she admitted.

"And that's why I'm taking a chance on these boys," Kaiden replied. "I can see the hunger in those boys' eyes. It's the same hunger I had at their age."

Ari smiled.

"And this is why you're so admired, Kai," she spoke to Kaiden as he drove.

"Yeah, yeah," he chuckled. "I'm just trying to leave a positive mark on this world for my wife and daughter when I leave here," Kaiden shrugged his shoulders. "The only thing that matters once they lower your casket is the impact that you've made on society. That's my concern: what mark will I leave here?" Kaiden finished as he continued to drive.

Ari nodded her head in agreement.

"You're absolutely right. But I know I'm not just speaking for myself when I say that you have been a blessing to all, Kai," she responded.

Kaiden chuckled.

"I'm just being me," he replied. "But trust me, *The Three Kingz* will be huge. If they come through and perform like they just did, I see great things coming about."

"Wait, but what about Lester's album? Aren't we going to focus on that?"

"We can do both," he slightly shrugged his shoulders. "Trust me, by the time they email me and they're set, Lester's album should be released, and the world should be buzzing."

Ari thought for a moment.

"So, what if they email you tomorrow?" she asked.

"Exactly," Kaiden replied.

Ari nodded in agreement.

"I get you, now," she spoke as she realized that Kaiden was saying they needed to hurry and finish Lester's album.

9

"We got all the lights set up?" Kaiden asked as Ari walked past him.

"All the lights and sound equipment are set," she spoke calmly.

"Where are we with refreshments?" he asked her.

"Kai, calm down," she chuckled. "K.P. has your back; just breathe," she smiled.

Kaiden inhaled and exhaled.

"You're right," he smiled.

Everyone was moving around rapidly to make sure Lester's listening party was a success.

"Where's my bride and princess?" Kaiden asked as he looked around for Samantha.

"They're on the way," Ari spoke. "I just got off the phone with Samantha."

"And what about Lester? How's he doing?" Kaiden asked as the two walked.

He picked up a bottle of water from the table and opened it.

"He's fine," Ari replied. "And these are for the guests," she chuckled. "This will be a success, you'll see," she finished.

Guests began to fill the room and Kaiden looked on as the security guards wanded everyone with the metal detector and patted them down.

"We're making sure *T.K.* Nation doesn't step foot in here, right?" he whispered to Ari as they watched the guests enter.

"Yes," she spoke. "The guards have been alerted that the *T.K.* Nation crew is to be denied entry."

"Keep your eyes peeled," Kaiden spoke. "I have a feeling that tonight will be a night we shan't soon forget," Kaiden advanced into another room.

Ari looked over the balcony and saw Francis, Emmanuel, and Zayne enter the building.

She pulled out her phone and sent Kaiden a text.

Ari: Kai, the 3 kings are here

Ari returned her phone to her pocket and walked down the stairs to greet the gentlemen at the door.

"You guys made it," she chuckled.

"We wouldn't miss this for the world," Francis spoke as his brothers were still in awe that they were speaking with Ari Love. Francis extended his hand for a handshake from Ari.

"I'm a hugger," she chuckled as she embraced Francis.

When they retreated, she hugged Emmanuel, and then Zayne.

"Kai-G is somewhere running around," she laughed, "but you all know he's being tight on cell phone usage and unauthorized photos and videos. The last thing we want is for the album to leak, so those phones must be powered off," she chuckled. "And if they're not, for the hardheaded folks, we have cell blockers all around this building which block all cellular communication, except to emergency services. Plus," she added, "security is on high alert, watching for those who may be using the devices."

"Completely understandable," Emmanuel spoke as he turned off his phone.

His brothers did the same.

Ari looked at her phone and saw a text from Kaiden.

Kaiden: Okay. Bring them over to section 105. I want to speak to them with the team. Prophet and Smoove are both over here.
Kaiden: do you see Samantha?
Ari: no sign of her yet

"Come on, guys," she spoke to the three gentlemen. "Follow me."
Ari led the group to the room that Kaiden was in.
The gentlemen entered the room.
"Kai, you remember *The Three Kingz,* right?" Ari asked Kaiden.
"I can't forget," Kaiden chuckled. "Glad you all could make it," he shook each of their hands.
"How are you all doing this evening?" Kaiden asked.
"We're great," Emmanuel spoke.
Emmanuel looked around in awe; he and his brothers were standing in front of their favorite artists.
"Better, now that we're here," Zayne spoke.
"I just wanted to introduce you all to the team," Kaiden responded. "You've already met Ari. This is B. Smoove and The Prophet," Kaiden introduced his artists.
"Nice to meet you all," Emmanuel spoke.
"Kai tells us you all stopped him in the parking lot," Byron stated.
"And that you all can deliver," Lester continued.
The three nodded their heads.

"Yeah, we saw the video of the performance," Byron spoke. "We're gonna put that shit to the test," he laughed before sipping his water.
The three looked at each other.
"Right now?" Emmanuel spoke.
"Nah," Byron spoke as he rose to his feet. "Right now, it's my boy's time to shine. But just know that we're watching you all," he gave a smile of encouragement.

"Mr. Green, Samantha has arrived with Kailyn. Christina and Isaias are also with them," one of the crew members spoke over the earpiece.

"Send them up. Section 105," he mentioned.

"Ladies, Kaiden would like for you all to come to section 105," the crew member spoke to the four of them.

Christina lightly rubbed her small baby bump.

"Good, because me and this little one need to rest," she chuckled.

Samantha rolled her eyes at Christina and chuckled.

"You're barely pregnant," she joked. "Have you heard from Trequan?"

"He's supposed to be here," Christina replied as she scanned the room for her boyfriend.

"Text his ass," Samantha scoffed. "He's gotta be somewhere close, right?" she asked.

"Yeah, girl," Christina laughed as she texted Trequan.

"Mommy, where's *Daa-yee*?" Kailyn asked Samantha.

"We're about to go see him now, babe," Samantha replied to the toddler.

Christina, Samantha, Isaias, and Kailyn walked with security behind a see-through wall where they saw the fans; all of whom were anxiously waiting to hear Lester perform.

"Excuse me," Christina spoke as she bumped into a fan.

The man lifted his head and under the cap revealed a familiar face.

"Well, well, well," he spoke with a slight laugh.

"Jordan," Christina spoke, slightly startled by his appearance.

"If it isn't the lovely Christina Parker and Samantha Williams," he smiled.

Christina had a severe weakness for Jordan's smile.

"What's up, shorty?" Jordan spoke to Isaias.

Isaias hid behind his mother but peeked at Jordan.

Jordan's build scared Isaias. The tattoos frightened him, as Jordan had them on his face, neck, and arms.

"He doesn't know, does he?" Jordan asked Christina with a slight look of disappointment.

"He knows," Christina replied. "You know he does," she rolled her eyes. "But he hasn't seen you in years; he doesn't know you," she finished.

"Why are you here, Jordan?" Samantha asked as she held Kailyn's hand.

Christina held Isaias' hand tightly.

Seeing Jordan brought memories of when Brandon appeared at the *No Turning Back* tour and shot Kaiden. A chill ran down her spine.

"Don't worry," he chuckled. "I'm not here to fight," he rolled his eyes. "It's actually kind of funny that I'm a big fan of *King Pin* and it's run by the same nigga I fought."

Christina looked at Samantha and spoke.

"So, you're here as a fan?"

"Exactamundo," he spoke. He glanced down and saw her stomach. "Another bun in the oven?"

Christina pulled her shawl together and closed it.

She didn't answer his question.

"You're still beautiful," he replied with a smile. "Something about the pregnancies that make you glow even more," he chuckled.

Christina rolled her eyes.

"You know I have a man, right?" she spoke.

"And you know the sky blue, right?" Jordan responded in a smart tone. "The fuck? I'm just making conversation. Not tryna hit on you. Shit," Jordan continued, "if I wanted to, I know I could still hit that shit."

Christina laughed.

"Is that what you think?" she asked.

"*Maybe if you were Kaiden,*" she thought, but she didn't speak it.

"Ladies, Kai-G is waiting," the security guard interjected.

"Come on, girl," Samantha spoke as she held Kailyn's hand and pulled her along.

"I'll see you around, Jordan," Christina spoke.

"Samantha," Jordan called.

Samantha looked over her shoulder.

"You're walking a little funny. Maybe you should get it checked out as well," he chuckled.

Samantha rolled her eyes and continued walking up the stairs with the security guards, Kailyn, Christina, and Isaias.

As they reached the top of the stairs, Samantha spoke.

"I don't have a good feeling about Jordan being here," she continued to hold Kailyn's hand as they all walked to the room.

"It is a little weird," Christina admitted. "But I don't think things will go sideways," she shrugged her shoulders.

"Just stay on guard," Samantha spoke. "We gotta tell Kaiden that he's here."

"We can do that," Christina responded. "Just so that he's aware, but I don't want to worry him."

They entered the room and Kailyn ran to her father.

"*Daa-yee!*" She exclaimed as she leaped into his arms.

Samantha's heart fluttered upon seeing this.

"There's my princess," he spoke as he kissed her cheek.

"Hey babe," Samantha gave him a kiss.

He put his hand around her waist.

"My queen," he smiled.

Samantha laid her head on his chest.

"What's up, Tina?" Kaiden greeted Christina.

"Hey Kai," she replied.

"Where's Tre?" He asked as he looked around.

"He's on the way," Christina answered as she looked at her phone. She looked at the screen inquisitively as a note was Air-dropped to her.

She opened it.

"*Yo Tina itz Jordan. Lock my number in,*" Jordan attached his number to the note.

Christina rolled her eyes and put her phone in her pocket.

"Well, let me know when he gets here," Kaiden spoke as he looked at his phone before returning it to his pocket.

"Bring it in, everyone," he gathered his team. "You, too," he spoke to *The Three Kings*.

The three brothers walked forward with pride.

"Everyone, bow your heads," Kaiden instructed.

Everyone bowed and Kaiden continued.

"Father, we are all gathered here today not because of the money, not because of the fame, and not because of the music; we are gathered here today because of family; we are all family. You have blessed us time and time again, and for that, we are forever grateful. Father, I come to you to ask you for your guidance and assistance during today's performance."

Samantha loved it when Kaiden said a prayer; she realized this was something he did quite often since the shooting. She got goosebumps as she listened to him.

"Everyone here in the venue has traveled some distance to see Brother Lester perform and release his highly anticipated album, and it would be wrong to take the credit for this. It is all because of you; you've granted the skills and the talent, so now I ask for your hands to keep us covered during this showing in order to keep everyone safe. If there are any signs of the devil present, get rid of them, Jesus. Positive energy only, and we give the power over to you," Kaiden continued.

Christina looked at Kaiden with a grin on her face.

"We give it all to you, Jesus," Kaiden uttered. "You're the reason everything is coming together, and we would be nowhere without you. We love you and we thank you, Father. In your name we pray, Amen," Kaiden finished.

"Amen," everyone spoke simultaneously.

"Amen," Kailyn spoke after everyone else and they laughed.

Christina ran her hands through Isaias' hair.

"Lester, go out there and kill it. This is your time to shine," Kaiden spoke. "You know *King Pin* has your back through it all," he gave a small pep-talk to Lester and picked up the golden microphone from the desk.

"Thanks, Boss," Lester spoke as he took the microphone.

The crowd was chanting 'Prophet' and Lester exited the room.

"We should go get our seats," Kaiden spoke to the team as Kailyn hugged him tightly.

As Ari, Byron, and The Three Kings exited the room, Christina noticed how Samantha was looking at her.

"Kai," Christina sighed.

"What's up?" he asked as he looked out of the window of the suite.

"Guess who we ran into on the way here," she chuckled as she tried to make light of the news.

"It wasn't Brandon, was it?" Kaiden emitted a small laugh.

Christina looked at him sternly.

"*How?*" she rolled her eyes. "He's dead."

"You sure about that?" Kaiden replied as he looked at the crowd.

He saw Lester walk onto the stage.

Samantha had goosebumps on her arm as Kaiden asked if they were sure that Brandon was dead.

"Yes, dummy," Christina shook her head. "I'm talking about this one's father," she ruffled through Isaias' hair.

Kaiden's smile never left his face.

After a few seconds of silence, he spoke.

"I'm not worried about that," he laughed. "You see that," he pointed to the window. "That's my artist out there performing for this huge crowd. Not too long ago, I thought this was a fantasy and was only a story you would hear about from big famous rappers. Sitting and dreaming 'man, we gotta be those niggas on TV; doing it big,' and now, it's happened."

Samantha walked closed and put her arm around her husband. "As long as I have love around me," he looked at Samantha and then at Kailyn, "I'm going to make it to the top. *King Pin* is going to make it, and I'm damn sure not about to let *anyone*, especially Jordan or Brandon, take that from me," Kaiden adjusted his *King Pin* hoodie.

A tear formed in Christina's eye and she wiped it away.

A few seconds of silence passed.
"Go on out there and kill it, babe," Samantha smiled as she took Kailyn from his arms.
"I'll see you in a bit," he kissed her on the lips and seemed to vanish as he exited the room.
Christina was silent as she held Isaias' hand tightly.
"Mommy, is everything okay?" he asked innocently as he noticed the tears in her eyes.
"Yes, baby," she answered.
"Call, Trequan," Samantha instructed after a few moments of silence.
***

"I want to thank everyone for coming out here and rocking with me," Lester spoke to the crowd.
The crowd chanted his name and his voice cracked.
"I gotta show mad love to my boy Kai-G; he's somewhere around here," Lester chuckled, "as well as my whole K.P. family. They believed in me even when I didn't believe in myself. They pushed me to get this album out and make it a memorable debut."

The audience roared as Lester continued to speak.

"And if you like what you just heard, make sure you go and cop '*The Prophecies*' next week when it drops. Tell your neighbors, friends, family, hell," Lester chuckled, "tell Donald Trump."
There was laughter from the audience and Christina couldn't help but laugh at his comment.

She felt as though it were a small jab at her for her previous views on Donald.

"I hope everyone's drive home is safe and I'll see y'all next time," Lester shouted over the microphone before walking backstage.

A member of the stage crew gave him a towel and he wiped his face.

Ari was the first to greet him backstage.

"That was epic!" she exclaimed.

"Thanks, Ari," he gave her a hug. "Where's everyone?"

The audience's commotion could still be heard from backstage and Lester put the towel around his neck.

"Come on," she led him to the room with the crew.

"That was tight," Kaiden spoke as he held Kailyn. "They're ready for the album to drop," he continued as he touched his daughter's hair.

Kailyn clapped her hands together.

"Thanks, Boss," Lester mentioned as he shook Kaiden's free hand. He tickled Kailyn's stomach.

"I'm glad you enjoyed it as well, little mama," he chuckled at Kailyn. "What's next?" Lester asked.

"Well," Kaiden chuckled, "I would say get back out and make some noise, but I think that's already been accomplished. K.P., huddle up. "Let's debrief," Kaiden projected.

Ari and Byron both came closer.

"Y'all, too," Kaiden spoke to Francis, Emmanuel, and Zayne.

The brothers approached with their heads held high.

Kaiden smiled.

"The album drops next Friday. We're going to do everything we can to make sure this is a success. Now," he cleared his throat, "because of tonight, our workload is 100 times easier. But that doesn't mean we can take our foot off the gas. Don't let go of this energy that we have; we're going to keep working and make this big," he put his arm around Samantha. "The show's just beginning."

10

Kaiden held Kailyn's hand as they crossed the street from the ice-cream parlor.

"Did you enjoy the ice cream, baby?" he spoke as she skipped merrily.

"Yes, *Daa-yee*," Kailyn squealed.

"I'm glad," Kaiden spoke as the two walked. "I gotta hurry up and get back," he looked at his phone.

He returned his phone to his pocket and picked Kailyn up.

"Come on, little one," he kissed her on the cheek and power-walked back to the house.

Samantha was sitting on the porch when they arrived.

"Look who's back," she chuckled as she rose to her feet.

"Sorry, babe," Kaiden started, "our little diva was indecisive as to what she wanted."

Samantha played with Kailyn's afro-ponytail.

"She just wants the best like her daddy," Samantha kissed him on the lips. "Ari, Smoove, and Lester just showed up. They're downstairs waiting on you," Samantha spoke as Kaiden led the way into the home.

"Thanks, babe. Where are we looking with the first- and second-week numbers for Lester?"

"Still rolling in," Samantha answered, "but so far, he's at 52-K units sold. At this rate, he's looking at having sold a little over 78 thousand copies for the first month."

"And we still have a few weeks to go," Kaiden chuckled.

Kaiden smiled at the piece of paper Samantha passed him. According to superstar producers, 78 thousand wouldn't be a large number, but to Kaiden, he was amazed at the number pushed by his artist on his debut album.

"Man, oh man, how quickly life changes," Kaiden smirked at the work.

"Remember, *you* did this," Samantha reminded him. "You made this happen."

Kaiden kissed Samantha on the lips and walked inside the home. Samantha led Kailyn upstairs to play with the babysitter. He walked down to the studio while holding a paper bag.

"We workin' hard, or hardly working down here?" Kaiden joked as he walked over to the table.

The artists all chuckled.

"You know we're hardly working," Byron joked.

Kaiden laughed and opened the paper bag, revealing the bottle of wine.

"I'll let it slide today," Kaiden chuckled. "Although, you hardly ever work," he joked with Byron.

Ari and Lester chuckled.

Byron shrugged his shoulders and laughed.

"Smoove, open that bag over there," Kaiden pointed to the bag on the table.

Byron opened the bag and pulled out a bottle of Hennessey and some wine coolers.

"Oh, you tryna get *lit* lit, huh?" Byron asked.

"This is to Lester," Kaiden smiled. "Celebration for him passing 50 thousand units in the first two weeks."
Ari applauded at the number.
"That's definitely something to celebrate. That's an astounding number, bro," she walked over and embraced him. "Don't stop."
"Yeah man, keep the fire alive," Byron spoke. "The fans will need to see more of you."
"I got you, man," Lester spoke.

Kaiden smiled at his artists and pulled out the red cups. He walked over to the table and poured each of them a small amount of Hennessey.
Samantha walked down the stairs and sat in the chair next to the mixer.
Lester's album was playing over the speakers.
"And," Kaiden started, "for the record," he chuckled, "us playing this album doesn't add to his streams. We have the master tracks stored locally, so the numbers you see for streaming, are coming from the fans."
Kaiden boasted at this accomplishment and felt he was in a position to do so.
"Guys, let's not forget to give the glory not only to God, but to this angel right here," he put his arm around Samantha. "This woman right here, she's my rock, and Lord knows she's keeping us alive. No one here works harder than her. Where would we be without her work?"
Everyone applauded Samantha.

Kaiden kissed her on the lips.
"I love you," he spoke to her.
"I love you, too," she smiled. "Let me help you with that, babe," Samantha uttered as she helped Kaiden with the cups.
"Thanks, babe."

"Any word from *T.K.* Nation lately?" Lester asked.

"None," Kaiden spoke. "And let's keep it that way. We don't need the negative energy flowing our way. We got a classic album out right now and we're going to roll on this positive wave."

Ari nodded in agreement.

The doorbell rang and the camera monitor automatically turned on.

Francis, Emmanuel, and Zayne stood at the door.

"I invited the Three Kingz over," Kaiden announced as they saw the three. "Let them partake in the celebration and let you all hear what they got."

He nodded his head and Samantha pressed a button near the mixer.

"Hey guys," she spoke over the microphone.

The men looked around to figure out where the voice was coming from.

Samantha laughed over the microphone.

"Come on in guys and follow the signs to the studio."

Samantha pressed another button and unlocked the door.

Francis, Emmanuel, and Zayne each walked into the home and followed signs to the studio.

Once they came to the door leading down the stairs, they laughed at the rules of the studio.

The three of them said a small prayer before walking to join the rest of the team.

"What's up, what's up?" Francis spoke to the team.

"My guys!" Kaiden exclaimed as he walked over and greeted the three. "Glad you all could make it."

"And miss this opportunity? We'd be pretty stupid to pass it up," Emmanuel responded.

"Check it out, we've got drinks and chips on the table; basically having an in-house celebration of The Prophet's album dropping."

The Three Kingz looked around the studio in awe.

"You all remember the team: Ari," Ari raised her hand; "Smoove," Byron gave a nod; "and The Prophet," Lester saluted the gentlemen.
"Nice to see you all again. And brother," Francis spoke to Lester, "congrats on the album. That's a classic, right there."
"I appreciate that man," Lester replied.

"Can't wait to hear what you all got for us," Samantha smiled. Kaiden walked over to his wife and put his arm around her.
"Gentlemen, allow me to introduce you to the backbone of *King Pin*. I know you thought it was me, huh?" Kaiden laughed. "My queen, Samantha Green," he kissed her on the cheek.
"Nice to meet you, Mrs. Green," Francis spoke.
"It's nice to meet the entire team," Zayne said.
"Mrs. Green?" Samantha smirked. "I love it, but it's too formal. Call me 'Sam'," she spoke to the men.

Kaiden continued.
"Momentarily, I'm going to let you all give it a go and perform for us," he looked around the studio. "Maybe let you all lay down a track if you're good for it."
This was a dream come true for The Three Kingz.
"Wow, man, this is amazing," Emmanuel replied. "We won't let you all down," he assured Kaiden and the team.
Kaiden nodded his head.
"You all go on and let loose; K.P., let's get to know these exquisite young men," Kaiden chuckled.
Kaiden and the crew were cleaning up when Byron commented on the brothers.
"Y'all know that shit you just did in there was cold," he spoke as he threw the plastic red cups in the garbage bag.
"That means a lot coming from you," Emmanuel spoke as he swept the chip crumbs into a pile. "My brothers and I want to thank you all for inviting us through."

"Nah, man," Kaiden started, "we are the ones who should be thanking you for blessing us with that performance," he smiled. "That was monumental."

The Three Kingz smiled as Kaiden complimented their work.

"I was once your age," he continued. "I know what hunger is, and you boys are definitely hungry. But, personally, I see that you all aren't only doing it for the fame; you all love the music."
The brothers nodded their heads in agreement.
"And today, the music is going to love you all back," Kaiden smirked as he looked at Ari.
Ari nodded her head in approval.

"It's late, guys," Ari spoke. "Go on, head home, and get some rest, but we'll invite you all back out soon."

The gentlemen were ecstatic, and it showed. They said their goodbyes to everyone and Kaiden walked them from the studio.

"Hey, man, I just want to say thank you all once again for coming through. It was an honor to have you."
"It was an honor to be here," Emmanuel spoke.
Kaiden nodded.
"Ari will be in touch with you all. Make sure you answer that phone," he laughed and walked back to the house.
"Got it," Zayne started.
The brothers couldn't believe they'd just performed for *King Pin*.
"Boss," he finished with a smile.
Kaiden walked back outside with a grin.
He reached into his pocket and pulled out a roll of hundred-dollar bills.
He unrolled them and gave each of the gentlemen seven.

"Your first payment for your work," he smirked. "You laid down those tracks and performed, you should be getting paid for it, right?"

The boys were speechless.

"Welcome to *King Pin*," Kaiden finished. "Ari will hit y'all up and let you know when to come through to finish signing."

Kaiden shook hands with each of them. They were still dumbfounded.

"Thank you," Emmanuel finally spoke.

"Get home safely," Kaiden replied as the brothers walked away.

He smiled and walked inside before closing the door.

Kaiden returned to the studio and looked at Byron.

Byron nodded and grinned.

"I'm getting in the booth. Arm me up," Kaiden said as he walked towards the recording booth.

He gave Samantha a quick kiss and entered the booth.

"Load up *The Kingz's* track. From the top."

"I got you, Boss," Byron spoke over the microphone.

Kaiden closed his eyes; he worked best when he freestyled with his work.

"Kai-G,
I give 'em blessings every time I touch the mic
Lookin' at my daughter always gets me hype
Listening to my artists, this shit feels so right
I'm 'bout to re-marry Samantha and just keep it tight
The love that we have is so damn monumental
Every time I smile, I'm thinkin' of all we went through
My scars, my pain, my vision, my failures, man this shit's been real
Sam's been there, through it all, so I know it must be special
Just checked off on the boxes next to these major Kings
With the help of my team, man it really seems
King Pin makin' this shit happen; signin' all these dreams
We gettin' out of debt, ay man, tell me who's next
Just dished out a couple stacks or maybe it was a couple checks

They see me checkin' people out, and it's a major threat
We growin', we expandin'
The world singin' our anthem
But hey, my nigga, Lester dropped his album, man go get that shit
The thing about the game is that it'll turn your friends against
you," he thought about Eddy and *T.K.* Nation.
Kaiden didn't want to make this a diss track, so he kept the references short.
"Realizing now, they'll eat with you and disassemble
Keep grindin', man, we haven't come close to our potential
That's why I'm doin' this shit, success is never accidental
K.P. leavin' heavy marks on everything we touch
Drop a verse, put it out, the world will eat it up
Get the blogs and the internet something to vibe to
And when Kailyn's older, she'll look back and say
"Damn, my dad was clutch."

Kaiden switched the flow.

" Whatever's mine is hers
And Sam, oh yes, it's yours
Always thinkin' of the future, 'cause shit, we had it rough," he returned to the previous flow.
"And this is a message for all of my people fightin'
Just keep your head, if you need some help, I'm always recitin'
I want you to win so keep on overwritin'
Don't think it's overreachin', if it's something you can believe in
If you're Black, you're never whack, a yo, just keep on fightin'."
Kaiden stopped rapping and listened to the instrumental through the headphones.

Ari, Byron, Lester, and Samantha were all in awe at the freestyle that Kaiden just rapped.
"Put their chorus right behind it and then their verses."
"They know this what you're up to?" Ari chuckled over the microphone.

"Hell nah," Kaiden laughed. "That's the beauty of it. Let's keep it a surprise."

Byron smirked and looked at the monitor.
Kaiden exited the booth and gave Samantha a kiss on the forehead.
"You and Kai will *always* be taken care of," he spoke with confidence. "Just do me a favor: never give up or let go of me, babe," he kissed her forehead.
Samantha got chills as she heard him speak.
She continued to rest on his chest and nodded her head slightly.

"I think we've got a hit with this, man," Byron spoke as he saved Kaiden's vocals.
"Let's keep this on the low for now," Kaiden replied as he kept an arm around Samantha.
Kaiden looked at Ari.
"Ari, as stated, I'm going to sign *The Kingz*," he started, "so, between you and my baby here," he kissed Samantha on the cheek, "get the paperwork together. Make them wait about a week before we call them back out."
Ari nodded her head in reply.
"Is there an advance?" Samantha questioned.
"We'll work out all the semantics later. Let's just get the process started," Kaiden looked at the clock on the wall. "Let's close shop for the night and we'll regroup tomorrow."
"This is going to be different," Byron chuckled as he grabbed his hoodie. "An R&B group with *K.P.*."
"It expands the horizon," Lester spoke. "And if they can deliver, mission accomplished."
"My exact thoughts," Kaiden added as they all pushed in the chairs. "Let's not sleep on this opportunity before *T.K. Nation* tries to swoop in."
The team headed for the stairs when Ari spoke.

"Kai, these boys idolize you. There's no way they would go to your competition. Trust me, I can see their desire to be part of the team."

Kaiden nodded his head and kept his arm around Samantha.

"Maybe you're right, but we don't want another situation like we had with Bishop."

The team reached the door.

"So, you and Sam just get the paperwork drawn up, okay?"

Ari nodded.

"I got you, Kai."

Ari hugged Kaiden and he shook hands with Byron and Lester.

"Y'all text me when you make it in."

The three walked to their vehicles, got inside, and drove off. Kaiden closed the door and picked Samantha up.

"You know I love you, right?" he asked her.

"I'm pretty sure I do," she smirked as she kept her hands around his neck.

"As long as you know," Kaiden smiled.

"I love you, too, Mr. Green," Samantha chuckled. "But you've given me a new assignment. Can't do this right now."

Kaiden frowned and lowered Samantha to the ground.

"Do you have to?" he whined and chuckled.

"Don't give me that look," Samantha laughed. "We can do that later."

Kaiden shook his head jokingly.

"Why don't you come over and help me, Boss?" she questioned as she walked over to the file cabinet.

"Sure, my queen," he responded as he walked over to her.

Samantha pulled out a large accordion folder with tabs for each of the artists. She pulled a form from the last slot and wrote 'The Three Kingz' on the application.

"Nah babe, we're going to change their name," Kaiden smiled. "These are men; no longer boys on the hunt. *Major Kings* is more like it."

Samantha smiled.

"If they agree with it, I say it's a good change," she agreed.

Samantha wrote the name on the application.

"You know, I've been thinking about this thing with Christina and Trequan," she continued. "I want you to avoid the drama at any and all costs," Samantha spoke as she filled out the application.

"3 of them, 100K," Kaiden said as she was filling out the contract amount. "I hear you, babe. Mentally, I'm in a space where nothing can get to me," he answered.

Samantha smiled as Kaiden spoke.

"The company can afford it, right?" he asked.

"I'm sure we have it sitting around in a vault somewhere," Samantha smirked. "Lester had a pretty successful launch, streams and downloads have skyrocketed since the feud with *T.K. Nation*; we got it, babe," she assured him.

"Just want to make sure we don't go broke trying to change lives," Kaiden responded. "I have to make sure you and Kailyn are good under any circumstances," he kissed her cheek.

"Babe, don't talk like that," Samantha replied. "As long as we have you, we are good."

Kaiden looked through the folder and nodded his head.

"I'm curious, why are you worried about Christina and Trequan?" he asked.

"Because babe. I mean, she's my best friend, don't get me wrong, but everywhere she goes, her past follows her. Remember Brandon? Now Jordan is popping up unexpectedly. What's next?"

Kaiden listened to Samantha and saw how tense she was getting. He put his hands on her shoulder.

"Babe, shh," he hushed her. "I'm not going anywhere, and I would *never* leave you and Kailyn. I refuse to let go of what we've built," he laid a kiss on her lips.

Chills flowed down Samantha's spine.

"I want to keep you here with me forever," she responded.

"Here, let's put this on hold," he spoke as he took the contract from her and moved it to the side.

Kaiden picked Samantha up and sat her on the desk; he began kissing her.

She threw her neck back as she ran her hands through his hair.

"I love you so much," a tear fell from her eye.

"I love you, too," he assured her while kissing her neck.

***

"Welcome to *King Pin*," Kaiden announced.

He shook Francis' hand.

The brothers were speechless as Kaiden and Samantha stood side-by-side.

Ari, Byron, and Lester sat in the chairs behind Kaiden and Samantha.

"Wait, are you serious right now?" Emmanuel spoke in awe.

"This is the future… your future. I wouldn't joke about something like that," Kaiden smiled.

The brothers were ecstatic.

"You put in the work to be here, are working your asses off to perfect your craft; you all deserve every bit of it."

"We won't let you down," Emmanuel replied.

Kaiden looked at Samantha and she nodded her head.

She slid the volume slider to a higher level and the audio started playing.

"Double X-L," James spoke over the radio. "We have the latest straight from *King Pin*. It's a completely new sound, but I like it," he chuckled.

The instrumental started and the brothers went wild.

"It gives off that 90's hip-hop and r&b vibe," James added. "These brothers go by *The Major Kingz*. What do you think?"

The song the brothers had previously recorded played over the speakers.

"Is that our song?" Francis asked as he heard Kaiden's verse.
"What better way to welcome you all into the group than with a song featuring none other than the big boss," Ari spoke with a smile.
The brothers were speechless as the song played.
"Now, this is just a trial," Kaiden said. "It's not guaranteed to get consistent airplay, but they're going to see how the audience responds and move accordingly."
"Thank you," Emmanuel spoke on behalf of all the brothers.

The song concluded and James came back on the air.
"Double X-L, we're back. That was **Motivation** by The Major Kingz featuring Kai-G. They're the latest addition to *King Pin* so what do you think of that track?" he asked. "It's a Double X-L Cool J exclusive, so you're not going to hear it anywhere else but here for the time being. Call us up and let us know if you were feeling that joint."

Kaiden smiled as he studied the brothers' faces.
He looked at his phone.

> ***Eddy: that shit was WEAK lol***

Kaiden shook his head at the text.

> ***Eddy: we recruitin' r&b niggas now. smh***

Kaiden replied.

> ***Kaiden: just stay in your lane. Don't come for these kings. Put your Bishop to work.***

Kaiden returned his phone to his pocket.

11

Samantha and Christina walked through the mall.
"Where's your security guard?" Christina chuckled.
"Girl, right here in my purse," Samantha laughed as she opened her purse. "I didn't feel like being followed by a guard today."
Christina saw the gun inside of the purse and shook her head.
"What?" Samantha started with a slight laugh. "My man just wants to make sure that I'm safe at all times. Especially when he's not around to protect me himself."
Christina chuckled at her friend.
"Man, you've got it good," she uttered.
"Everything that glitters ain't gold," Samantha spoke. "It's hard being the wife of a superstar."
"Please," Christina rolled her eyes. "Tell me all about your struggles," she scoffed.

Samantha looked at Christina as they walked.
"Seriously?" she asked. "you're telling me it's normal to not be able to go anywhere without security of some sort?"
"I would kill to have security around me 25-8," Christina laughed.
"Okay," Samantha kissed her teeth. "Want to balance the books?" she questioned.

"Will I get insight into K.P.'s financials?" Christina laughed.
"You would," Samantha laughed heartily.

"How are things otherwise?" Christina and Samantha continued to walk towards the food court.
"We're managing," Samantha spoke as she humbled the accomplishments. "Lester's album is doing well and that's where the buzz is... right where we want it," she added.

Christina reached in her purse and pulled out her debit card as they approached Subway.
"That's what's up," she remarked.

Christina studied the menu.
"You know what you want?" Christina asked. "It's on me."
Samantha shook her head.
"Girl, put that card away," she remarked as she pulled out her debit card. "I got you."
Christina raised an eyebrow.
"No, you put yours away. I got this," Christina rolled her eyes.
"Tina, I'm not about to play with you," Samantha replied.

Christina burst into laughter.
"Shit, okay, I'll save my money then," she returned her card to her purse.
Samantha shook her head.
"You are something else," she laughed at her friend.
They ordered their food and walked over to an open table to take a seat.
As they ate, they were approached by Jordan and one of his friends.

"What's good Tina? Sammy-Sam?" he asked as he sat down across from them.
Samantha rolled her eyes.
Christina never took her eyes from her sandwich.

"What, Jordan?" Christina rolled her eyes.

"Is that any way to talk to the father of your child?"

"Correction, your ass is a sperm donor," Christina rebutted. "Just because you helped make him doesn't mean you're a father. Any idiot can make a baby."

"Now I'm a idiot?" Jordan scoffed.

"My point exactly," Christina replied. "You're *an* idiot."

She took another bite of her sandwich.

"Where's my son?" Jordan asked.

"*My* son," Christina stressed, "is minding his business and in his skin."

"You talk a lot of shit," Jordan rose to his feet.

Christina and Samantha rose at the same time as Jordan.

Jordan observed the two ladies as they rose simultaneously.

His friend looked at him.

"I think you're gonna have an issue getting this bitch in check," he laughed.

"Bitch?!" Christina questioned in disbelief.

"Calm down, Tina," Samantha stated to her friend.

"Nah, La'Darius, I got this hoe right where she needs to be," Jordan smirked at Christina.

"Girl, let's go," Christina glared at Jordan. "It's smelling a little bit like broke niggas over here."

Samantha chuckled at her friend's comment. She nodded her head and proceeded to wrap her sandwich.

Christina and Samantha both put their sandwiches into the bag and Christina brushed past Jordan.

Jordan smirked as the ladies walked past him.

Christina and Samantha left the mall and entered the parking lot.

Jordan and La'Darius jogged to catch up to them.

"Tina, you need to talk to me," Jordan asserted.

"Talk to you about what?" Christina asked as she continued to walk.

"My son fo' one," Jordan began as they trailed the ladies. "And about us getting back together to be a family fo' my son."
"Jordan, I don't have shit to say to you. You haven't given me anything for Isaias since he was born, and we will *never* get back together. I let the shit go and so should you," Christina responded as they continued walking.

Jordan glared at Christina and grabbed her arm.
She stopped and looked at him.
Samantha remembered she had the gun in her purse.
"Jordan, I'm not that bitch that I used to be," Christina started. "Today is a new day; I'm not scared of you like I used to be. I'm not trapped behind insecurities; I'm a free spirit, boo," she finished. "Now, this free spirit says, 'get your muthafuckin' hands off me'," Christina ripped her arm away from Jordan.
"Don't let this bitch get you fucked up," Jordan uttered as he referred to Samantha. "Stop showing yo' ass to me," he grabbed her arms again and tightened his grip.
Christina chuckled.
"Sam, please tell me this jig-a-boo didn't grab me again."
Samantha could see the situation was escalating. She pulled out her phone.

Samantha (to Kaiden): babe, get to the mall ASAP. Jordan is

La'Darius slapped the phone out of Samantha's hand, but in the process of doing so, he sent the message.

"Put that shit down," he uttered.
"I'm sorry, who the fuck are you?" Samantha spoke aggressively. "And what gives you the fucking authority to touch me or my shit."
"You's a silly bitch, you must not have heard about me," La'Darius smirked and lifted his shirt to reveal a gun.
"You think I'm scared of that?" Samantha asked as she put her hand inside her purse. "Try me, nigga."

La'Darius looked at Samantha's purse.
***
Kaiden saw Samantha's text.

"Shit," he spoke aloud. "Man, we gotta go," he spoke to Byron.

"What's going on?" Byron asked as he put on his jacket.

"Christina's ex is at the mall fuckin' with them," he hurried. "Do me a favor. Call Dennis and rally up the troops. Send them to the mall."

"Fuck," Byron spoke. "Just when you think we've caught a break," he dialed Dennis' number.

"Samantha's got a piece on her, but let's hope it doesn't escalate to the point where she has to use it."

"Dennis, we have a 9-1-1 at Woodfield Mall," Byron spoke.

"Subjects are Samantha Green and Christina Parker."

"We're familiar with Mrs. Green," Dennis spoke. "But not with Ms. Parker. I assume the two are together," he typed a few words into his computer and rose to his feet.

"Affirmative," Byron spoke professionally.

"We're on it. I'm taking the lead and will have my men on site in ten minutes."

"Thank you," Byron ended the call.

"Man, I'm not sure why this nigga is still on this tip. Let the shit go," Kaiden and Byron walked out of the studio. "I completely understand that's his son, but what has he ever done for him?" Kaiden and Byron got into Kaiden's vehicle and they drove away.
***
Samantha looked at her phone on the ground and noticed the screen was shattered.

Christina tried to rip her arm away from Jordan, but his grip was too tight.

"Bro, do you know who her husband is?" Jordan asked as he held onto Christina's arm. "He's a muthafucka," he scoffed.

"I don't give no fucks," La'Darius added. "I'll put a hot one through this bitch and her husband."

"High profile nigga, you sure you want to take that risk?" Jordan asked. "You'd be better off robbing the bitch than killing her."

Jordan realized it was too late to de-escalate things.
Samantha looked at Jordan and then at Christina.
She saw Christina was in pain.

Pedestrians in the parking lot were looking on as the drama unfolded. Many were rushing to get into the mall in case things escalated any further.

"Jordan, let Tina go," Samantha stated; she never removed her hand from the hammer of the gun in her purse.
"Nah, fuck that. This bitch is going to give me answers."
"Answers about what?" Christina questioned as she squirmed.
"You know, boo," he kissed her cheek.
Christina wanted to fight back, but she didn't want to risk her unborn child.

"The fuck is her husband?" La'Darius questioned.
Samantha looked at Jordan sternly. Jordan smirked before replying.
"You ever heard of Kai-G?" he asked La'Darius.
"The rapper?!" La'Darius questioned. "Bro, you telling me you know his fuckin' woman?"
La'Darius felt he'd hit the jacK.P.ot in coming across Samantha.
"Yo, run everything you got now, bitch," he spoke to Samantha as he pulled the gun from his waistband.
Samantha pulled the gun from her purse.
"You sure you want to do that?" she asked.

The onlookers hurried once they saw the weapons drawn. There were screams as many entered the mall. Many pedestrians called 9-1-1 and alerted mall security.

"Yo' pretty ass probably don't even know how to use that shit," La'Darius laughed. "Put it down before someone gets hurt."
"Me and my husband go to the range regularly. I don't miss," Samantha assured him.

La'Darius glared at her.

Two black SUVs pulled into the parking lot and the men jumped out.
Dennis, Alonzo, Gregory, and James all approached the crowd with their guns aimed.
"Protect the package," Dennis called as they approached the ladies.
Jordan and La'Darius saw the men approaching.
"Yo," Jordan whispered. "Chill with that shit," he knew Kaiden had sent the men and what they were capable of.
"Nah, fuck that," La'Darius spoke.
As Dennis, Alonzo, Gregory, and James approached the group, they informed the pedestrians in their vehicles to remain in the car but to stay low.

"Flank 'em," Dennis spoke over his earpiece.
Each of them approached from different sides with their weapons aimed.

La'Darius saw the men approaching and looked at Jordan.
"I told you," Jordan stated as he pulled Christina closer to him and tightened his grip.
Jordan wasn't about to let his friend show him up nor was he going to back down.
Kaiden drove into the parking lot with Byron.
"Shit, man," Byron spoke as he saw the events unfold.
"Just keep your head," Kaiden replied.
The two quickly unloaded from the car.
Kaiden and Byron trotted over to the group.

"Mrs. Green," Dennis called. "Lower your weapon," he instructed calmly.
Samantha looked at Dennis.
"Instruct Jordan to let Christina go and La'Darius to lower his," she shouted.

Christina looked at the security guards and placed her hand on her stomach.

"Proceed with caution," Dennis instructed as he saw noticed Christina was pregnant.

Kaiden saw the gun aimed at Samantha and spaced out.
In an instant, he ran in and tackled La'Darius to the ground.
"Mr. Green," Dennis shouted as the two tussled on the pavement.
"Babe!" Samantha shouted as she put the gun in her purse.
Samantha ran in, but Dennis intercepted.
"Stay back, Mrs. Green. We got this."
He spoke over his earpiece. "Add subjects: Kaiden Green and Byron Jones."
Byron ran in and intervened with the fight.
"Boss," he shouted.
Alonzo walked closer with his firearm aimed at Jordan.
Gregory and James both hurried in to protect Kaiden.

Pedestrians in the parking lot were running to get in the mall and were hurrying to get into their vehicles.

"Let her go," Alonzo shouted to Jordan.
"Do I have a weapon?!" Jordan questioned. "Y'all can put the guns away."
Alonzo approached slowly and extended an arm towards Christina.
"Reaching out to target," Alonzo reported over his earpiece.
Christina reached an arm out to Alonzo and anticipated a tighter grip from Jordan.
Jordan released her and she hurried over to Dennis.
"Target one is safe," Alonzo reported. "On your knees," he instructed Jordan.
Jordan gave a dirty glance to Alonzo.
"I don't get on my knees for no man," Jordan scoffed.
He looked over at La'Darius and saw he was still wrestling with Kaiden.

He saw Byron trying to separate them but noticed Gregory and James both attacking La'Darius as he wrestled with Kaiden. "Fuck," Jordan whispered.

In a sudden movement, he lunged in to help his friend.
However, instead of fighting the men, he tried to separate everyone.
Alonzo couldn't determine what Jordan was doing; he was trained to protect the target by any means necessary.
"I have a shot," he reported over his earpiece.
"Do not fire your weapon!" Dennis spoke as he held Samantha to prevent her from interfering.

Byron grabbed Kaiden's shoulders and pulled him away from La'Darius.
Kaiden's shirt was torn and his pants were slightly ripped near the knees.
Byron tightened his grip so that Kaiden couldn't break free.
"She's good, Boss. See?" Byron nodded his head at Samantha.
The adrenaline was rushing through Kaiden's body, but it seemed to subside as he made eye contact with Samantha.

Gregory and James brought La'Darius and Jordan to their feet.
Alonzo kept his gun aimed and his finger on the trigger.
Byron walked Kaiden over to Samantha and released him. Kaiden embraced Samantha.
"Targets apprehended," Dennis spoke over his earpiece. "What actions would you like taken?" he asked Kaiden.
Kaiden looked at Christina and Samantha.

"He's a threat," Christina blurted.
Christina noticed Samantha's purse to the right of her.
"Bitch, what?!" Jordan asserted as his anger built as he heard Christina speak.
Christina flinched at his aggression.

He tried to break free from Gregory's hold; Gregory tightened his grip on Jordan's arms.

"Loosen that shit, man," Jordan scowled.

Dennis slowly approached and reached down to retrieve La'Darius' gun.

"Do with them what you will," Kaiden uttered as he held Samantha tightly.

"No!" Christina reached in Samantha's purse and pulled out the gun.

Samantha felt Christina's hand reach in her purse and tried to stop her from pulling the gun out, but her reaction was too late.

She aimed it at Jordan and walked closer to him.

"Miss Parker," Dennis spoke as he approached Christina with his gun aimed.

"Christina!" Kaiden shouted.

"Tina, stop," Samantha spoke to her friend as she released her embrace from Kaiden.

Dennis kept his hands on his weapon but slowly lowered the firearm.

He touched Christina's shoulder.

"He has to pay for what he's done," she insisted.

She remembered the emotional abuse she'd undergone while dating Jordan, the arguments, the physical abuse, and his fight with Kaiden.

She fired a shot at Jordan.

He fell to the ground as blood rushed from his chest.

"Bro!" La'Darius called.

Jordan didn't reply.

"You fucking bitch!" La'Darius asserted.

Alonzo kept his weapon aimed at La'Darius.

"Give me a reason," he threatened.

"Miss Parker," Dennis grabbed for the gun. "Let it go!" he instructed.

Christina kept a firm hold on the gun as the two tussled for it.

As they struggled, another shot rang out.

Looks of shock and awe crossed everyone's face; especially Kaiden's.

Samantha fell to her knees and held her stomach.

She collapsed and laid on the ground.

"Baby!" Kaiden shouted as he rushed over to her.

He held Samantha's head up.

Christina dropped the weapon as she realized she'd shot her friend.

Dennis held Christina's arms.

"We need two ambos in the west parking lot of Woodfield Mall," Alonzo spoke over his earpiece.

"Samantha?" Christina called softly.

Kaiden rocked Samantha slowly and kept her head elevated.

He looked at Christina with tears in his eyes.

She couldn't help but cry softly as she'd realized what she'd done.

"Keep your eyes open, babe," Kaiden whispered to Samantha as he tried to fight the tears.

"All this time," Samantha whispered, "I feared you leaving me and Kailyn," she coughed. "I didn't think you'd lose me. You know, we never recorded that song," she smiled.

Kaiden smiled.

"Babe, we'll always be together. Neither of us is going anywhere. I'll never let go," he stroked her hair. "And we have plenty of time to record the song; this isn't the end. I love you."

Samantha got goosebumps on her arms.

"I love you, too," Samantha whispered.

Kaiden leaned forward and kissed her on the lips.

***

12

As Kaiden's lips left hers, Samantha abruptly woke up.
"Damn, it felt so real," she silently cried. "Why couldn't it have
been me?"
Sweat dripped from her forehead as she looked over to Kailyn.
She saw her daughter hugging her teddy bear.
Samantha walked over and kissed Kailyn on the forehead before
walking to the washroom.
She turned on the water and washed her face as tears fell from
her face.

"You would leave me when I need you most," she chuckled as she
spoke aloud; she hoped Kaiden would hear her. "I'm trying to
keep everything together, but we're all struggling, Kai. Although
K.P. is thriving, the artists aren't feeling the motivation without
your touch."
Samantha grabbed a Kleenex and wiped her nose.
"I know you can see that Kailyn is growing like a weed; every day,
I can see she's more and more of your daughter," she looked at the
open doorway. "I can see it in her mannerisms and the things she
does on a day-to-day basis."

She felt a cool breeze alongside her face, although there were no open windows and no fans were on.

"It's just hard, and Kai, I miss you," she cried.
She turned off the water and walked to the door and noticed the covers on her bed folded over; she knew when she got up, she didn't leave them that way.
She looked around and slowly walked around the room to investigate.
Kailyn was sleeping in her bed with a smile on her face and she tightly held the bear.
Samantha put her hand on Kailyn's head before bending down to kiss her.
She walked back over to her bed and got inside.
She clinched the pillow tightly before closing her eyes.
She felt the breeze across her face once more before falling asleep.

The next morning, she dressed herself and Kailyn, and the two of them left the home. She sat in the limo with Kailyn and smiled while looking at her daughter.
"So young and innocent. Not a care in the world," Samantha chuckled to herself as Kailyn played with the window.
Her phone rang and she answered the call on the first ring.
"Samantha, girl, where are you?" Ari spoke.
"Kailyn and I are on the way. Is everything set there?"
"Yes, the guests are rolling in. Security is covering all angles and is keeping everything secure."
"Good," Samantha replied. She looked out the window in dismay.
"We're about ten minutes away. Please keep order there, girl. Sorry, we're running late."
"That's understandable," Ari sympathized with Samantha as she looked at the cutout of Kaiden.
A few tears fell from Ari's face.
"Be safe," her voice cracked before hanging up the phone.

Samantha put her phone on the chair next to her and opened her purse. She pulled out a Kleenex and wiped her eyes.

"Mommy, why are you crying?" Kailyn noticed the tears.

She moved closer to her mother.

'God, you look and act just like your Daddy,' Samantha thought to herself. "It's nothing baby."

She hugged Kailyn tightly and rested her face on the child's head.

The limo arrived at the location and Ari walked to the door with the security guards.

They opened the door and helped Samantha out of the vehicle.

She wore her dark sunglasses and kept her hands on Kailyn's shoulders.

Kailyn looked ahead and spoke excitedly.

"Mommy look!" she squealed. "There's *Daa-yee*!" she pointed to the cutout. "*Daa-yee*!" she called.

Samantha couldn't stop the tears from falling as she saw her daughter's excitement.

Ari bent down and picked Kailyn up.

Although tears filled her eyes, she did her best to keep a smile on her face.

"Hey, Kailyn, I have something to show you inside," she forced the words out of her mouth.

"Can't *Daa-yee* come with us?" Kailyn innocently asked as Ari walked to the door.

"Daddy's busy right now, baby girl. But he wanted me to show you this," she spoke as she walked ahead of security to the basement of the building.

As Samantha entered the building, she heard Kaiden's voice playing over the speakers. *So In Love* was playing and the words were chilling to her as she listened to him rap over the vocals.

She looked ahead and saw a banner that read: 'The Memorial for Kaiden Green'. Underneath, it read: 'I Was Trapped, But Now I'm Free. Time to Let Go'.

A picture of Kaiden, Samantha, and Kailyn was the image chosen for the memorial.

The fans that sat in the congregation rose to their feet as Samantha entered the room with security.
There were security guards at each row, and they kept their arms extended as Samantha was escorted down the aisle.
Mama Green rose to her feet and walked towards her daughter-in-law as she reached the front.
Samantha looked at Kaiden's body inside of the casket and Samantha could hardly stand.
"Kai, why'd you have to leave me like this?" she spoke to his body. "You know that Kailyn and I both need you."
She bent down and kissed him on the cheek and could have sworn she heard a voice whisper, 'I promise. I'll never let go of us'.

The way they'd made up his body was nearly perfect, and he appeared to be sleeping as opposed to deceased. There wasn't a single blemish on his face and no expressions could be made out. However, Samantha could have sworn she saw him tighten his eyelids and smile slightly.

Mama Green extended her arms and embraced Samantha.
The tears were falling uncontrollably as she sobbed into Mama Green's shoulder.
Byron walked over to them and put his arms around them. He, too, wore dark sunglasses.
"Stop," Samantha spoke as she cried harder. "I need him so much."
"It will be okay, Sam," Byron tried to comfort her while fighting his own tears.
Kaiden's grandmother put her hand on Samantha's lap and wept silently. His grandfather kept his arm around his grandmother and kept a stern look on his face.
"Where's my baby?" Samantha asked about Kailyn.

"Ari took her downstairs to be with the other children," Byron uttered. "Quite a few of these fans who came brought children with them."

Thinking of her daughter growing up without a father made her cry even harder.

Christina and Trequan entered the hall hand-in-hand. She wiped a few tears from her eyes.

Trequan held his head high as they approached the front row. Christina extended a hand and touched Kaiden and the tears flowed down her face onto his body.

"Why, God?" she silently uttered.

Trequan hugged Christina.

"Come on, babe," he motioned for her to embrace Samantha.

She walked towards her best friend and Samantha rose to her feet.

Samantha embraced Christina tightly.

Samantha released her embrace with Christina, and they kissed each other on the cheek.

She gave Trequan a slight embrace before retreating.

"Thank you all for coming," she spoke to them.

Trequan nodded his head and put his hand on Christina's back for her to sit in the second row behind Samantha.

He put his hand on Samantha's shoulder when they sat while keeping his arm wrapped around Christina.

Ari came back upstairs, and the security guards blocked off all the aisles as she made her way to the front. She sat next to Samantha.

"Kailyn is downstairs playing with the other children and Isaias," Ari assured her.

"Thanks, Ari," Samantha silently spoke.

"If everyone would take their seats and settle down, we would like to get started," the pastor spoke.

Samantha took Ari's hand in her left hand and held Mama Green's hand in the right. She gripped both hands tightly.

"Ladies and gentlemen, we are here this morning to celebrate the life of Kaiden Bryson Green."

Samantha had a weird feeling in her stomach as the pastor spoke. It reminded her of the dream she'd previously encountered that she told Kaiden about.
She couldn't tell what was real at that point.
"What the fuck?" she thought to herself.
***
Samantha and Ari sat on the steps of the stage as Kailyn and Isaias ran around.
Fans and family had each left the repast and only a few people remained; including the artists that Kaiden worked with, Samantha, Kailyn, Christina, Trequan, and Isaias. The security officers were also present to protect Samantha, the children, and the artists.
Samantha hung her head and Ari kept her hand on Samantha's back.
"I don't know how the hell we're going to do this," Samantha admitted. "*King Pin*, the house, the cars, the studio; everything. It feels like everything's going to fall apart without him," she spoke to Ari.
"It's going to be hard," Ari confirmed, "but you know I have your back, girl. With anything you may need." Ari looked at Kailyn.
"You know that I love you both. I've damn near appointed myself as her god-mother," she chuckled lightly.

"It's fitting," Samantha laughed. "You're like one to her."
"Yeah girl, plus, K.P. is raking in the dough right now. All of this will be paid for before the night is over." Ari still looked in the direction of Kailyn and Isaias.
"And I promise you, we're not stopping because of this. We're going to go ten times harder, but we need for you to not quit," she encouraged Samantha. "We need you more than anything, now. More importantly, Kailyn needs you."

"It's just hard," Samantha spoke. "And you know Kailyn adored him. She truly loves him; how do I break it to her?"
Ari sympathized.
"I don't know," she smiled as she looked at Kailyn. "Kids are so innocent, and Kailyn is a doll. If you need my help with her in any way, I got you, girl."
Samantha nodded her head slightly.
"Well, the best thing to do is what Kaiden would do: get back to work," she forced a smile. "We keep pushing."
Ari patted her on the back.
Samantha rose to her feet.
"Then, we have our game plan. We keep Kaiden's legacy alive," she stretched her arms out.
Ari rose and gave Samantha a warm embrace.
"I got you," she assured her.

Samantha smiled and directed her attention to Kailyn. They both walked towards her.
"Come on, little girl, it's time to go," Samantha spoke as she extended her hand to Kailyn.
"Okay," Kailyn responded as she and Isaias stopped running in circles.
She ran up to the life-like cutout of Kaiden.
She hugged the cutout of her father.
"Bye, *Daa-yee*. See you soon. I love you."
Kailyn waved at the cutout.

Samantha broke into tears upon seeing this.
Kailyn stood on her tiptoes and kissed the cutout on the stomach.

13

"No!" Samantha shouted as she woke up from her sleep.
She was breathing very heavily as she looked around the room.
Kailyn was laying in her crib, and she heard faint beeping.
The television was on, but it was muted, so there was no audio
emitting from the machine.

Samantha rose to her feet and walked over to Kailyn. She touched
the infant and kissed her on the cheek.
"My sweet baby girl," she whispered.
"Babe, what's wrong," Kaiden asked.
Samantha walked over to the bed and touched his face.
"Is this real?" she questioned aloud.
"Is what real?" Kaiden chuckled.
She touched his chest, his arms, his abs, and then his legs.
"Are you feeling okay, babe?" he asked. "I know I'm the one in this
hospital bed, but we may need for them to pull a bed up right next
to me and have you get some rest."

She couldn't believe it.
"Babe, don't bullshit me!" she squealed silently.
"What's wrong?" Kaiden asked, confusedly.

Samantha thought for a moment and recalled past events.
***

"Kaiden, please don't leave me," Samantha pleaded. "Kailyn is going to need her father and I'm going to need my husband by my side."

Samantha looked at the monitors and saw the heart rate increase to 135 beats-per-minute. Seconds later, the heart rate dropped to the previous speed of 78 beats-per-minute. It increased once more to 120 before dropping to 78.

"Kai, stop playing with me," she teared up as she rested on his chest.

Several nurses ran into the room.

"What's going on?" Samantha asked.

"He's coding. Ma'am, we're going to have to ask you to step outside."

"What does that even mean?" she frantically asked.

"As soon as we have more answers, the doctor will be out to get you," the nurse rushed.

Samantha looked through the windows and saw the nurse checking his I.V. before a different nurse closed the curtain.

She texted Christina and told her that he was coding, before returning to the waiting room.

She sat in the waiting room with Mama Green, Kaiden's grandparents, Byron, Ari, and C-Sharp.

Lester walked through the doors, rushing.

"Smoove, how is he?! I came as soon as I heard what happened," he panicked.

Byron nodded his head towards Samantha. Samantha held Mama Green's hand and rested her head on Mama Green's shoulder.

Ari kept a hand on Samantha's back; she could feel that Samantha was jittery.

Ari looked at Lester and shook her head for him not to ask any questions right now.

He took a seat in the area and clasped his hands together.

Mama Green stroked Samantha's hair before speaking.
"Get some rest, baby. Worrying isn't going to help anything. We've prayed and now it's in God's hands."
Samantha slightly nodded her head and Mama Green kissed her on the forehead.
Samantha closed her eyes.
***

She hugged Kaiden tightly; she forgot about his injuries for a moment. Multiple tears fell from her eyes.

"Damn, babe," Kaiden coughed weakly.
Samantha released her grip and sat on the bed next to Kaiden.
"Are you really here?" she asked.
"Not after that bear hug," he joked. "Almost took me out, girl," he smiled.
"Prove it to me," she insisted.
Kaiden displayed a puzzled look. He had no idea what she was referencing or what was going on.

"Babe, are you feeling okay?"
"I'm not crazy," she breathed heavily; she was overjoyed that he was there beside her. She planted kisses on his cheek.
"Before I wake up and you're not there," she cried silently. "I'm going to take advantage."
"Baby, what's going on? I'm right here and thanks to the wonderful team of doctors, I'm not going anywhere any time soon," he chuckled lightly.
"Oh God," tears flowed down her face and she cried aloud as she rose to her feet and paced the floor.

Kaiden looked at her inquisitively.
"Come here," he motioned for her to come closer to him. "Lay right here beside me."
Samantha walked closer to Kaiden and he did his best to move over in the bed.

She sat in the bed before rotating her body to a lying position. She faced Kaiden and put her hand on his chest; she was careful with the I.V. tube and different probes on his body.

He wrapped his arms around her.

"I know this has to be uncomfortable for you," Kaiden chuckled.

Tears continued to flow down her eyes.

"This is perfect," she silently cried. "I just want to see you and be held for a while, babe."

Kaiden kissed her forehead.

"I thought I'd lost you," she spoke silently.

"You're not going to lose me," he assured her. "I'm right here."

"I just had the wildest and most vivid dream."

Kaiden chuckled slightly.

"I can imagine so," he replied. "The doctors told me that you were so frantic that, although illegal, they had to subdue you in some way. You refused to leave the hospital, and they couldn't risk you ripping these probes from my body," Kaiden lightly shook his head.

He looked at his arm; Samantha stroked it lightly.

"You've been sleeping for almost a week," Kaiden smirked. "And, to prevent you from waking up, they added more sedative every time you started squirming and motioning like you were about to wake up. So, they had to keep you under."

Samantha's eyes widened.

She recalled every time she had goosebumps in her dream or felt chills. She figured that had to be the medication entering her veins.

"That explains the detailed dream that I just had."

"Well, babe, we have nothing but time. Tell me all about it."

She stroked his chest.

"Well, for one, stay away from Eddy," she laughed lightly.

"He's bad news, huh? How worried should I be?" he chuckled.

"Very," Samantha joked, yet was serious. "He recruited Jada, her new boyfriend, and a new artist to try to tear you down."

"Now you know I'm truly not worried about that, right? Do you know who I am babe," Kaiden scoffed as he held Samantha tighter.

"I know," she kissed him on the cheek.

"Tell me more about this dream," Kaiden spoke out of curiosity.

Samantha readjusted her laying position before speaking.

She proceeded to tell him about The Three Kingz, Lester's debut album and how it would perform, the way Eddy pitted them against one another; she even spoke on Christina moving around the corner from them.

"Seem like shit is going to get crazy," he laughed lightly. "You ready for the battle?"

Samantha kissed him on the lips.

"For you," she started, "I'll go to battle, war... maybe even the grave."

"Don't talk like that, babe," he continued. "No one's going anywhere except out of the hospital and to continue with this unfinished business."

Samantha was silent for a moment.

"I love you, Kaiden Bryson Green."

"I love you, too," he replied.

She snuggled her head in his chest and closed her eyes.

14

Two years later, Kaiden stood tall in the mirror and adjusted his shirt.

Ethan stood behind him and brushed his hair.

"My boy is about to take that big step. Damn, you've come far," he took a step over to the desk.

Kaiden smiled in the mirror.

"Man, after getting shot and almost losing my life, I've realized that there's no time like the present. Why should I continue putting off what I can do today?"

Ethan nodded in agreement.

"Plus," Kaiden continued, "this way, if something were to happen to me, Kailyn and Samantha would be set financially, and they wouldn't have any worries."

"Bruh," Ethan started and turned to look at Kaiden, "stop with that shit. Nothing is going to happen to you," he shook his head.

"You are about to marry a gorgeous woman and you all have an adorable daughter. You own a multimillion-dollar record label with some of the best hitters on your team. Stop this talk about death."

Kaiden turned and faced Ethan.

"I'm being for real right now, man," he scratched his head. "Tomorrow isn't promised, and I'm a provider before anything else. As long as Samantha and Kailyn are good, I couldn't give a damn about anything else."

Byron walked into the room.
"You ready, Boss?" he asked as he greeted Kaiden.
"I wish he would get ready," Ethan answered. "He keeps talking about death."
Byron's smirk left his face.
"Boss, you've been through a lot, and no one can deny that, but it's how you handle those adversities that say everything," Byron spoke. "And thus far, you've done a hell of a good job."

Kaiden cleared his throat.
"It's hard," he admitted. "Running the label, ensuring Samantha and Kailyn are straight," he rubbed his rib, "this marriage. It's a lot and starts to weigh down on ya' boy," he chuckled slightly.
"You are already a great father," Ethan spoke, "and I know you're going to be a great husband to Samantha. You're already a strong support system and are doing a hell of a job keeping everything under wraps."
"Keep being great, man," Byron spoke. "Everything else will fall into place."
Cody rushed in the door and was fixing his collar.

"I heard someone's getting married," Cody spoke.
"Yo' ass is always running late," Kaiden chuckled.
"Better late than never," Cody made sure his cufflinks were secured.
Kaiden laughed at Cody.
"Man, it's something wrong with you," he smirked.
"Nothing wrong with me, baby boy."

Kaiden smiled at his best men.

"I appreciate everything you all are doing for me and have done. It means a lot."

"Don't even sweat it, my nigga," Cody finished.

"Let's get you over that broom," Byron spoke. "So, you and Sam can spend that gorgeous honeymoon doing whatever your heart desires."

"Definitely traveling," Kaiden immediately replied. "Already have it planned out; hitting 7 countries across two months."

"You guys are going to be doing a lot of moving," Lester spoke.

"You damn right," Kaiden chuckled. "So, can you all hold K.P. down in my absence?"

"We got you," Byron spoke as he patted his back.

***

Samantha adjusted her dress as Christina assisted.

A tear fell down her eye.

"It's really happening," Samantha smiled.

Ari wiped the tear from her eye with a Kleenex.

"Girl, we can't be messing up your makeup before the magic words," she chuckled. "Not to mention I just spent over two hours perfecting everything," she giggled.

Samantha chuckled at Ari.

"I can't believe this day is finally here," she squealed silently.

"Better believe it," Christina replied as she secured the dress.

"Today's the day you officially take Kaiden off the market," she forced a slight smile.

Samantha noticed the hint of sarcasm in Christina's voice but ignored it.

"I appreciate you all for being here for this day," Samantha continued.

"Don't mention it," Ari answered as she walked over to the counter and picked up the white corsage. "Here girl," she spoke.

Samantha held out her arm and Ari put the piece on her.

"Man, if Kaiden doesn't realize how lucky he is, I'm not sure what to say," Ari laughed. "You are glowing, girl."

Samantha chuckled at Ari.

"Thanks, girl," she answered.

She looked at Christina and noticed a look of disappointment.

"Um, Ari, go out there for me and check on the guests. Make sure everything is in order and we're good to go," she found a reason for her to leave the room.

Ari started to walk out, and Samantha continued.

"Oh, and make sure the Kings are here," she called out.

"I got you, girl," Ari closed the door behind her.

"Alright, girl, give it to me straight," Samantha spoke to Christina.

"What's going on with you?" she sat down on the stool.

Christina sighed.

"It's just seeing you and Kaiden getting ready to tie the knot," she began to confess to her friend. "About to 'jump the broom' if you will," she chuckled.

Samantha looked at her friend sternly. She knew there was something Christina had to get off her chest.

Christina continued.

"You have it all," she started. "You have the success, a beautiful little girl, a wonderful man," Christina paused. "You're living *my* dream."

"Tina," Samantha groaned, "this is perhaps the biggest day of my life, and I invited you to be my bridesmaid because you're my girl, but don't give me this spill today."

"Kaiden was mine and you snatched him from under me," Christina whined.

Samantha raised an eyebrow.

"Please elaborate on how I took Kaiden from under you. Because, if I remember correctly, it was your actions with your convict boyfriend that made you lose Kaiden, not me."

Samantha reflected on when she and Christina were in the parking lot of the mall and Jordan approached them.

"Matter-of-fact, I damn near pleaded for you not to fuck with Jordan. But you don't listen, Tina," Samantha spoke. "You didn't listen to me when I told you that dating a man eleven years older than you wouldn't end well, you didn't listen to me when I told you to tell him the truth about Isaias, you didn't listen when I told you not to mess around on Kaiden because you had a beautiful thing going, and you damn sure didn't listen when I told you not to screw up twice because Kaiden could see your bullshit." Christina retaliated.

"Don't even go there," she responded. "You knew how I felt about Kaiden, and then you go and sleep with him?" Christina scoffed. "He was emotional, and I was emotional at the time, and you took advantage of him," Christina kept her tone down to a low mumble. "He came to my hotel after he caught you cheating. If you cared about him the way you say you did, you wouldn't have even put him in that situation," Samantha replied.
"It was the heat of the moment," Christina rebutted. "Don't try to use that shit against me."
"Shit happens," Samantha continued, "I get it. But what about the second time?" she questioned. "Kaiden agreed to try again and to see where things would go, yet you continued to talk to Trequan. You don't listen, Tina."
"I did some fucked up shit," Christina confessed. "I made a mistake."
"Well, that mistake ended up costing you a lifetime," she rolled her eyes, slightly.

She looked at Christina and saw the tears in her eyes.
"I'm sorry, Tina," Samantha showed compassion. "That was harsh."
"You don't have to apologize," Christina spoke as she rose to her feet. "It's the truth," Christina walked over to the mirror and adjusted her hair.
Christina looked in the mirror and adjusted her dress over her baby bump. She smiled at the sight of it.
"I'm not going to lie, Sam; I'm honestly happy for you," Christina cleared her throat and rubbed her stomach.

Samantha stood and walked over to Christina.

"Isaias and this little one right here are what keep me smiling. Regardless of the life I have, or had, these two and Trequan keep me pushing; I just can't help but think about what could have been if I hadn't been foolish."

"Tina, you have it good," Samantha put her arm around her best friend. "You have a good man who's doing a hell of a good job raising Isaias and taking care of you. Honestly, you're not going to find too many men that are willing to take care of someone else's child and put up with your shit," Samantha chuckled.

Christina looked at her friend and laughed.

"Don't look at me like that," Samantha scoffed. "You're my girl, but I'm going to call you on your shit."

Christina shook her head slightly and smiled.

Samantha faced Christina and extended her arms for an embrace. Christina accepted.

"Listen to me this time," Samantha chuckled. "Don't screw this up. God has given you another chance at unconditional love."

Christina smiled and rolled her eyes at her best friend.

"I love you, girl," Christina embraced Samantha.

"I love you, too," Samantha replied.

Seconds later, they retreated from the hug.

"Now," Christina spoke, "let's get you over that broom."

***

Armed security guards were covering each entrance to the church.

Kaiden stood tall as he observed the guests sitting in their chairs. He was amazed at how many people came out to celebrate his wedding.

Not once did he ever think he would be in a position where he could say he had such a dynamic impact on people's lives.

Standing next to him were his best men: Ethan, Cody, and Byron. They all wore tuxedos with bow-ties. Each of them had cufflinks of their initials, engraved with a diamond: a gift from Kaiden to them.

Directly across from them were the bridesmaids: Christina, Samantha's older sister, Desiré, and Ari.

Kaiden sighed.

He scanned the room and saw his mother and grandparents sitting in the front row beside Samantha's mother and Trequan. His mother blew him a kiss and tears filled her eyes.

He smiled at his mother and cleared his throat.

He looked to his left and saw The Major Kingz in front of three microphones.

He smirked at the fact that some of the things Samantha dreamed would happen, actually came true: The Kingz, Eddy's attempt to take his team down by signing three new artists and releasing diss tracks, Lester having a successful debut album. Her prediction about Christina partially came true; she moved to Indiana, which wasn't too far from them, but it wasn't around the corner, either. Perhaps while she was sedated, she entered the spiritual realm and connected to the higher power.

The brothers all stood proud to be getting ready to sing at Kaiden's wedding.

Kaiden continued to scan the room and his eyes landed on Jordan. It seems like Christina's past continued to follow him, even though he wasn't with her.

"Heads up," he whispered to his best men. "Row 12, seat A," he observed the row and seat Jordan sat in.

"What about him?" Ethan whispered.

"Christina's ex and Isaias' father," he continued.

"The nigga you fought?" Cody asked in a low tone.

"Yes. It seems like her sins continue to follow me," Kaiden spoke through his teeth while keeping a smile on his face.

"Don't worry about him, man," Byron spoke as all the best men looked directly at Jordan. "You want him out?"

Kaiden continued to smile and sighed.

"Nah, it's cool. Let him stay but keep an eye on him."

"I'll let security know," Byron spoke as he adjusted his bowtie and walked away from the others.

Ethan put a hand on Kaiden's shoulder.

"We got you, bro," he said.

Byron walked over to one of the security guards and alerted them of the situation. The guard relayed the message to the others and Byron returned to his position behind Kaiden.

A soft, melodic instrumental began, and Emmanuel spoke over the microphone.

"Ladies and gentlemen, it's an honor to be standing before you at this gathering," he began. "My name is Emmanuel, and behind me are my brothers: Francis and Zayne."

The brothers nodded their heads.

"And we are 'The Three Kingz'."

Francis began to harmonize as Zayne spoke to the instrumental.

"*Ooh yeah. Girl, you know I love you. You've been here with me since day one. Allow me this opportunity to show you how much you mean to me.*"

Emmanuel began to sing to the instrumental as both Kailyn and Isaias came walking down the aisle.

Kailyn was the flower girl and Isaias was the ring bearer.

She had a flower crown around her hair and her hair was pinned up neatly. She had a solid white dress with white roses across the top.

She held the basket of roses in one hand and tossed the petals with the other.

Isaias wore a tuxedo with black dress shoes. He was practically Kaiden and the groomsmen's twin.

Kaiden smiled as they both walked down the aisle in unison.

"*And girl, I, I need you,*" Emmanuel sung along with his brothers.

Samantha turned the corner and walked down the aisle with her father.

She walked slowly down the aisle as tears filled her eyes; it was happening.

She was about to marry the man she'd fallen head-over-heels for. Kaiden proved to not only be a great father and provider, but he also proved to be a protector and a great potential husband.

Kaiden inhaled deeply and exhaled as Samantha got closer to him; his heart was racing and felt as though it would beat from his chest.

"*Baby, I love you. Be my wife, make me proud, say it loud...*" Francis adlibbed.

"*I love youuuuuuu*," the brothers harmonized and finished.

The audience applauded and Samantha and her father stood side-by-side.

The brothers took a slight bow and stepped away from the microphones and took their designated seats.

Kaiden looked at Samantha in awe. He couldn't believe he was moments away from solidifying their union.

"Good morning, brothers and sisters," the pastor began as the congregation quieted to a whisper.

"I am looking out in the audience and I see a lot of people here today," he chuckled. "I expect to see all of you back here on Sunday."

The audience laughed at his comment.

"But seriously, marriage is a beautiful thing. And," he inhaled deeply, "it can only work when a man and woman both put in the effort to make it work," he stressed.

"Speak on, Pastor," Kaiden's aunt shouted.

"I see you, sister," the pastor replied.

"Isn't she on divorce number four?" Ethan whispered to Kaiden.

Kaiden stifled his laughter and covered it by clearing his throat.

"I am Pastor Steve McCray and I was called by sister Samantha to join these two in holy matrimony, and I had to accept. I hopped on a plane and flew over here from Forks, Washington... over 2,000 miles away, just to be here today. I love this young lady as if she were my daughter."

Samantha continued to cry tears of joy as she held her father's hand and looked at Kaiden.

Kaiden looked Samantha in her eyes.

"Marriage is a beautiful thing and I am praying for these two as they get ready to take that next step."

Ethan, Cody, and Byron kept their hands interlocked as they kept Jordan in their peripheral vision.

"Who is here to give this beautiful young lady to this handsome young man?" the pastor questioned.

"I am," Samantha's father spoke. "Her father."

He looked at Kaiden sternly and extended his hand for a handshake.

Kaiden firmly took Samantha's father's hand in his and shook it.

"With this shake," her father began, "I am handing my daughter over to you. Always keep her and my granddaughter safe and protected. Make sure they have what they need, and if you ever aren't able to do something, you can come to me for guidance, son. Don't ever feel like you have to have it all figured out or go at it alone," he finished.

Kaiden smiled slightly and replied.

"Thank you. Your daughter is in good hands," Kaiden turned the handshake into an embrace.

Samantha's father patted Kaiden on his back and stepped down. He returned to his seat next to her mother.

Kaiden took Samantha's hands in his; this was it.

"I have been told that both the bride and groom have prepared their own vows that they would like to exchange," the pastor recited.

He looked at Kaiden.

Tears filled Kaiden's eyes as he stared at Samantha.

He reached in his sportscoat and pulled out a piece of paper.
"Samantha Williams," he began, "You are the perfect idea of what a woman should be. Not only a woman, but a mother, wife, and best friend."

Christina smiled as a tear fell from her eye. She put her hand on Samantha's back.

"You have been there for me since the beginning," Kaiden spoke. "The circumstances that brought us together were wild," he chuckled, and Samantha chuckled as well, "but you have always had my back."

Christina slightly rolled her eyes.

Samantha's eyes were full of tears as she smiled at Kaiden. She used a Kleenex and dabbed his eyes.

"See what I mean?" he laughed.

The audience laughed along.

"In a dark room, you light the way, and your positive spirit is enough to brighten any situation. The support you've given me is second-to-none; I can come to you about anything and I know you will always have my back, no matter what."

The tears began to roll down his face as he spoke.

"Samantha, we have a beautiful daughter together and we are terrific parents to her," they both looked over at Kailyn. "And I know she will always be taken care of."

More tears accumulated on Kaiden's face and Samantha mouthed out 'I love you'.

Kaiden's voice cracked.

"Samantha, I love you with all of my heart, and I can't wait for the wonderful, Pastor McCray, to utter those magical words; I couldn't be more ecstatic to be able to call you my wife."

Kaiden tried to hold back his tears but he couldn't help letting them fall.

As he sobbed silently, his groomsmen stood tall and broke the formation they were in. They each put a hand on his shoulder.

"Take your time, Kai," his mother shouted with tears in her eyes.

The audience applauded at Kaiden's tears to show their support.

The groomsmen patted him on his back and returned to his original formation.

"You are moments away from being my wife," Kaiden managed to continue. "And I honestly want this more than anything in the world. All the money in the world couldn't compare to what's about to occur."

Samantha teared up more as she saw Kaiden was full of tears. This was the moment she'd always wanted. She couldn't wait to become Kaiden's wife and make it official.

"The world doesn't know it yet," Kaiden continued, "but the fact that you're carrying my seed and we're about to make Kailyn a big sister is monumental to me."
The audience gasped and applauded at the news.

Christina was happy, yet a bit envious of her best friend; not because she was marrying Kaiden, but because she was getting married before her.
All they'd ever spoken about as children, was finding their one true love, discovering the true meaning of happiness, having some children, and growing old with one person — and Samantha had found that.
Christina teared up as she saw Kaiden crying.
Samantha's smile grew wider.

"I'm sorry, Pastor," Kaiden continued, "can you just say the words?" he chuckled as he wiped his eyes with his handkerchief.
The audience laughed.
"What about me?" Samantha chuckled.
"The first argument, brothers and sisters," Pastor McCray joked, and the audience laughed along, as did Kaiden and Samantha.

"Kaiden, you are the man I've always wanted," Samantha began with a huge smile on her face.

She touched Kaiden's cheek as the tears flowed down his face.

"The man I've always dreamed of becoming one with. The man I've always wanted to have children with. It's you," she smiled.

"Honestly, it's always been you."

Samantha's eyes welled with tears.

"You are an amazing man, Kai. Amazing to your brand, amazing to the artists, amazing to me, and more importantly, amazing to our daughter."

Kaiden couldn't help but interject.

"You mean *our. Our* brand; what's mine is yours," he smiled as he used his handkerchief on her.

"Yes, *ours*," she corrected. "Kaiden, you have always been a good man and I have always seen it. Honestly," she began, "I fell in love with you the moment I met you... physically, that is," she added.

Christina kept a smile on her face as Samantha spoke.

Kaiden smiled but made eye contact with Christina for a split second.

Christina slightly nodded her head and continued to stand tall.

"Kaiden Bryson Green, I love you more than life itself," Samantha's tears began to fall uncontrollably. "I give myself to you, and I will do my best to make you as proud as you've made me."

Kaiden exhaled as Samantha continued.

"I promise to give you all of me — my mind, heart, and soul. My love for you won't ever die, even in the afterlife."

Kailyn walked over to her mother and father and put her hands up while holding the basket of rose petals.

Kaiden smiled as he bent down and picked her up.

Samantha chuckled slightly and the audience applauded Kailyn.

"*Daa-yee*," Kailyn spoke as she looked at Kaiden. She looked at Samantha.

"Mommy," she added.

Samantha kissed Kailyn on the cheek.

"You will always have my heart," Kaiden replied. "You, this little one right here," he snuggled Kailyn, "and the little one growing within you, have my heart and are my entire world. I love you, Samantha Williams," Kaiden spoke.

The audience applauded and rose to their feet; Samantha's bridesmaids all had tears in their eyes.

Kailyn smiled and clapped her hands together as Kaiden held her.

"That was beautiful," Pastor McCray spoke moments later once the audience died down. "Do you, Kaiden Bryson Green, take the lovely Samantha Williams to be your lawfully wedded wife? To have and to hold, for better or for worse, for richer or for poorer, till death do you part?"

Kaiden looked at Samantha dreamily and answered.

"No," he shocked the crowd.

There were gasps of shock.

"We're not parting after death; this love is forever, and I'll never let go," Kaiden smiled.

"Allow me to rephrase," Pastor McCray chuckled. "For richer and for poorer, until you become one in the afterlife?"

Kaiden nodded his head.

"I wouldn't be here for any other reason," Kaiden replied. "I do."

"And do you, Samantha Williams, take this fine young gentleman, Kaiden Bryson Green, to be your lawfully wedded husband? To have and to hold, for better and worse, for richer and for poorer, until you become one in the afterlife?" he asked Samantha.

Samantha looked at her bridesmaids in the order that they were lined up behind her: Christina, Desiré, and Ari.

"Go on, girl," Christina mouthed out.

She looked at Kaiden once more.

"Kaiden, you have made me the happiest woman alive and I can't wait to spend the rest of my life with you," she spoke with tears in her eyes. "I do," she answered the pastor.

"Go on and exchange rings and utter the words 'with this ring, I thee wed,'," Pastor McCray spoke.

Kaiden squatted down to Isaias and got the ring from the casing.
"Congratulations, Kaiden," Isaias spoke clearly.
"My man," Kaiden nudged him with a smile.
Isaias smiled at Kaiden.

Samantha held her bouquet of flowers in one hand and looked at Isaias.
He smiled a huge smile.
"We couldn't have done this without you," she assured Isaias.
"I love you, Auntie Sam," he spoke.
"I love you, too, Isaias," she replied as she got the ring from him.
She kissed him on the cheek.
She rose to her feet and Kaiden removed her engagement ring. He placed the band on her finger and put the engagement ring back in place.
"With this ring, I thee wed," Kaiden spoke confidently.
Samantha was glowing as she put Kaiden's ring on his finger.
She could hardly get the words out of her mouth as she was crying uncontrollably.
"Kaiden, with this ring, I thee wed," she managed to speak.

Pastor McCray nodded his head and smiled. He continued.

"Then, by the power vested in me by the state of Illinois, I..."
Kaiden didn't wait for the pastor to finish.
He leaned in and kissed Samantha and the crowd applauded ferociously.
The audience rose to their feet while applauding.
Pastor McCray chuckled.
"I now pronounce you husband and wife. Go on and finish kissing your bride," he finished.
Byron, Cody, and Ethan applauded as they greeted each other and patted Kaiden on the back.

Samantha and Kaiden both shed tears as they cried, and Kailyn giggled.

Kaiden and Samantha's parents' eyes were both filled with tears as he kissed his bride.

Neither of them wanted the moment to end.

"I love you," Kaiden spoke.

"I love you, too," Samantha replied.

"Brothers and sister, Mr. and Mrs. Kaiden Bryson Green," Pastor McCray spoke, and the audience cheered and applauded louder.

"Wait, wait, wait," Ethan spoke as Kaiden and Samantha got ready to step down.

Samantha looked at Kaiden and smiled.

Byron passed Ethan a broomstick and he placed it on the floor.

Kaiden and Samantha both chuckled.

Kaiden shook his head at Ethan and smiled.

"I told you I'd get you over this broom," Ethan answered.

"My boy," Kaiden said.

Kaiden held Kailyn in one arm and had Samantha's hand in the other.

The two of them jumped over the broomstick and the photographer seemed to capture a picture at the perfect moment.

Kaiden returned Kailyn to the floor and she stood beside Isaias.

"Kaiden, over here," the photographer called.

He held Samantha's hand firmly as Isaias and Kailyn stood in front of them.

The second photographer took a picture.

"Beautiful," he replied.

The audience remained on their feet as they applauded the newlyweds.

Kailyn and Isaias took the lead and were arm-in-arm.

Kailyn threw rose petals on the floor as they led Kaiden and Samantha to the back of the church.

The groomsmen and bridesmaids each interlocked arms as they followed Kaiden and Samantha: Ethan and Christina, Cody and Desiré, and Byron and Ari.

As they reached the row Jordan was in, Isaias stopped in his tracks.

Kaiden saw the fear and trauma flowing through Isaias' body as he saw Jordan.

Kaiden put his hand on Isaias' shoulder.

"Come on, little man," Kaiden whispered to Isaias as he never took his eyes off Jordan.

Jordan smirked as Isaias refused to move.

"What's up, son?" Jordan spoke to Isaias.

Isaias turned and hid behind Kaiden. Kailyn was confused.

"*Daa-yee*?" she questioned.

Kaiden picked up Kailyn and Samantha held his hand tighter.

The audience looked on as the newlyweds stopped walking. They knew something was wrong.

"Jordan, not today," Kaiden spoke. "Let's keep the peace, okay?"

Kaiden held Samantha's hand. "Come on, little man," he spoke to Isaias. "It's okay."

Isaias peeked from behind Kaiden.

Dennis and Gregory walked in Kaiden's direction, as did Trequan.

"Nigga, don't you remember me beating your ass back in Washington over that bitch behind you?" he spoke as he referenced Christina.

She rolled her eyes and attempted to break formation to cover her son, but Ethan locked his arm around hers.

She looked at him and he nodded his head 'no'.

"Let's keep it all peaceful," he whispered to her. "Kaiden will handle this."

Christina obliged but was a little worried.

"No disrespect, I'm happy for you, but I'm not going to act like everything's all good between us. I'm just here to see my son," Jordan continued.

"Today is not the day for this," Samantha tugged at his coat sleeve.
"I know, babe, and I promise I'm going to get this handled immediately."
Dennis and Gregory approached and stood in front of the wedding guests; they were directly in front of Kailyn and were eye-to-eye with Jordan.
"What the fuck do y'all want?" Jordan emphasized.
"Please leave the premises immediately and we won't have to use force against you," Dennis responded gruffly.
Jordan eyed the two men up and down.
"You got security, huh Kaiden?" Jordan smirked. "Take it easy gentlemen; I come in peace."
"Your presence is no longer welcomed," Kaiden interjected.
"Please see yourself out."

Trequan reached the wedding guests, made his way to the front of the line, and spoke to Jordan.
"Look, this is my guy's wedding day, you know what I'm saying, and I'm not even going to cause a scene," he whispered through his teeth, "although I do want to beat the shit out of you for laying your hands on a woman," he looked at Christina. "*My* woman," he stressed.
"I'm shaking in my boots," Jordan sarcastically remarked.
Jordan looked around and saw how he was outnumbered by the guards, Trequan, Kaiden, and his groomsmen.
"If shit's going to pop off, I would have brought my piece," he forced a laugh. "Really, gentlemen, I come in peace. Every other fan can come, why can't I?" he uttered.

Kaiden stared at him blankly.
"You really want to do this?" he asked with a dark tone.
***
A tap on the wine glass silenced the room.
"Can I get everyone's attention?" Christina spoke.
Kaiden held Samantha's hand tightly as they both looked in her direction.

"Hi everyone, I'm Christina Parker; many of you have probably heard about me," she slightly shook her head.

"What is she doing?" Samantha whispered to Kaiden.

"This is *your* friend," he lightly laughed.

"Yeah, and it's *your* ex," Samantha bit back with a chuckle.

"Touché," Kaiden replied with a smirk.

Christina held her glass and stood next to Trequan.

"The bride and I go way back," she smiled as she looked at Samantha. "It seems like just the other day we were children talking about how we wanted our lives to turn out. Now, I'm here at your wedding, and I couldn't be more ecstatic," she cleared her throat.

Samantha nodded her head.

"Sam, you have taught me so much," Christina said. "You have taught me to be a better woman. I remember I used to be this wild child who was just out there," she had flashbacks of her and Brandon. "No one could control me."

"That's true," Samantha spoke aloud to her friend.

"Yeah, I know," Christina laughed. "But I've watched you. All along, I've been watching you. To keep it one hundred with you, I was always a little envious of you."

Samantha raised her eyebrows.

"You've always had everything; beauty, brains, class — I aspired to be like you," Christina wiped her eye. "And now, you're married to this great man. Girl, you're truly living the dream," she chuckled.

She looked over at the children.

"Kailyn is beautiful," Christina continued. "You and your husband are doing a wonderful job of raising her. Not to mention, she and Isaias get along so well," she smiled at her son as he sat with the other children.

"Sam," she continued, "you are who I want to be like when I grow up, even though we're only a few months apart in age," she laughed.

"When you told me that you were pregnant with Kaiden's child, part of me wanted to explode with rage," she admitted, "and I think that showed. But deep down, I was a little upset."

Kaiden kept his hand on top of Samantha's.

"Not even upset," she corrected. "I was jealous. You molded Kaiden into an entirely new man," Christina confessed her feelings, "and you changed the way he looked at a lot of things. And, I guess I was a little jealous that I couldn't be the one to do that."

Christina teared up.

"Girl, I am so proud of you," she added. "I am proud of everything that you've ever done, and I'm ecstatic that you're carrying another little Kaiden," she laughed lightly. "It gives me a chance to start all over and be an aunt to your new one."

Samantha smiled and a few tears accumulated in her eyes.

"I was jealous of you, Sam, and I'm at the point where I'm not too proud to admit it," she admitted. "You had it all, and I wanted what you had. I wanted your life, baby girl. And even when I had it," she made eye contact with Kaiden, "I didn't know how to appreciate it and took it for granted."

The tears rolled down her cheek as she thought about how she'd messed around with Jordan and even attempted to rekindle the flame.

Christina cleared her throat and wiped her tears.

"A wise woman once told me that I didn't listen," she chuckled as she recollected on the previous conversation, "and that God has given me another shot at love," she looked at Trequan and smiled. "Well, this time, I'm going to take that wise woman's advice; not only for me but for my son and this little one growing inside of me," Christina looked back at Samantha.

Kaiden started to raise his glass.

"And, to the groom," she added.

He lowered his glass slowly.

"Babe, get her off the mic," Kaiden joked.

"You," she started as she chose her words carefully. "I want to start by saying thank you for everything you've ever done for me. Not only for me, but my beautiful son, Isaias, and my gorgeous man, Trequan."

Christina chuckled and the audience chuckled with her.

Christina sighed.

"As many of you already know, I'm sure, Kaiden and I used to date."

"What is she doing?" he whispered to Samantha.

"I don't know but we're about to shut this shit down right now," Samantha rose to her feet.

"I know what you're up to, Sam," Christina projected. "Please, let me get this off my chest," she teared up a little more.

Kaiden put his hand on Samantha's back and she lowered into the chair.

"Kaiden was a great man. No, not was, he *is* a great man. Throughout the course of our relationship, I wanted to be able to have my cake and to eat it too," she continued, "so, I did the unthinkable: I cheated," Christina spoke.

"Yep, here it goes," Samantha slightly shook her head.

The crowd was confused as to why she was providing this information.

"You all know the guy from the wedding?" she asked rhetorically. "That was my convict ex-boyfriend whom I chose to mess around with. Which, as I look back, was very, *very*, childish of me."

Trequan looked on sternly as she spoke as she could feel his eyes looking at her.

"I'm saying all of this to say that as I look back, I see the man Kaiden was and the man he's molded into now. And this wonderful man you all see today, is the work of Mrs. Samantha Green."

The crowded applauded lightly.

"You all may or may not remember, but Kaiden did the unthinkable, and for it, I'm forever indebted to him," she teared up even harder. "He saved my son's life."

The audience gasped slightly.

"It was my fault, I know," Christina scoffed, "but he took a bullet — multiple bullets — to save my son and his daughter from another one of my exes; he's dead to me now, literally."

Kaiden nodded his head.

"And that was a very humble move. To think that he would even risk his life for my son after everything that happened between us... but," she added, "I guess that says a lot about his character and who he is as a man." Christina took a sip of water. "Kaiden *always* puts others' needs before his; I'm sure K.P. can attest to this. And he's all about giving back."

Kaiden smiled lightly.

Christina smiled at him and looked at the clock on the wall.

"I don't want to take any more time than I'm allotted," Christina joked as she picked up her champagne glass. "It's only sparkling apple juice, guys," she laughed with the audience. "Here's to the bride and groom," she concluded. "May you all live a lifetime and beyond, of happiness and success. May your love prosper and rise above all things. I love you guys."

Christina's eyes were full of tears at this point.

Everyone in the crowd raised their glass and toasted the air. They sipped the champagne before applauding Christina.

Samantha mouthed out to Christina, 'I love you, too,' and Kaiden smiled.

He nodded his head as he kept his hand around Samantha's waist.

Christina returned to her seat and the crowd gave her a standing ovation.

***

Kaiden and Samantha stood side-by-side as some of the remaining guests came over and conversed with them.

"Thank you for coming," Kaiden shook hands with one of the guests.

"You gotta let me know, when's that album of yours dropping?" the guest chuckled.

"Soon, man. Soon," Kaiden remarked. "I'm going to take this much-needed honeymoon-slash-vacation with my bride. And then, I'll focus on work."

"I feel you," the guest nodded his head. "Congrats again, man," he patted Kaiden on his shoulder before walking away.

Kaiden looked at Samantha and smiled.

"What?" she giggled.

"You are the luckiest woman alive," Kaiden replied. "And I vow to keep you the happiest."

He kissed her on the lips.

Christina approached the two of them slowly.

"Save some for the honeymoon," she joked.

"We will," Samantha smirked. "And more."

"T-M-I," Christina laughed.

Kaiden smiled at Christina and held Samantha.

"That was a beautiful speech you gave," he said.

"It was from the heart," she admitted. "Samantha, hold on to him," Christina remarked. "He's a keeper."

Christina smiled at Kaiden.

She was finally at peace with everything that happened. Christina realized she couldn't remain trapped with fantasizing what could have been; rather, she had to move forward and let go to get a full understanding as to why things were the way they were.

"Kaiden, thank you," Christina stated. "For everything."

"There's no need to thank me, Tina," Kaiden replied. "I'm just doing what I was sent here to do."

"Yeah, I know," Christina chuckled. "Be great and take over the world."

"One song at a time," Kaiden finished with a laugh.

Samantha kept her hand on his chest.

"What's next for the great Christina?" Samantha asked.

"Well, the first thing is to drop this little one," Christina smiled and rubbed her stomach. "And then, I don't know. Probably going to take the big leap like you all did."

Kaiden raised an eyebrow. He kissed Samantha on the cheek and spoke.

"I'm going to be right back, babe."

"Okay, babe."

He walked over to Trequan and Samantha continued to speak with Christina.

"Tre, can I rap with you for a second?"

Trequan studied Kaiden and nodded his head.

"What's going on?"

"Take that step," Kaiden suggested.

Trequan looked over to Christina.

He laughed lightly.

"I'm serious, man. We're not promised tomorrow, and I see you're an excellent father to Isaias, boyfriend to her, and you're going to be extravagant to your newborn."

Trequan smirked before speaking.

"She is a great woman," he began. He looked Kaiden in his eyes. "I want to thank you for loving her the way you did."

Kaiden nodded his head.

"In the beginning, you were all she spoke about. And man," he cleared his throat, "I'm not going to lie, I hated you for a while because of it."

He and Kaiden laughed.

"But no," he continued, "you taught her what it means to love, and I can't deny that. To be honest, I don't know how you put up with her shit for so long," Trequan laughed.

"She's a piece of work," Kaiden joked, "but she's worth it," he admitted. "Take that step, man," he reiterated. "Man-to-man, I see your greatness and potential. And I know she sees it as well," he looked in the direction of Samantha and Christina.

"Respect, bro," Trequan spoke as he and Kaiden sipped their drinks.

Trequan looked at the clock before speaking again.

"Let me go get this girl so we can head out."

"Let me walk with you all," Kaiden suggested as they walked over to the women.

Christina and Samantha looked at the men as they approached.

"Look at these fine men coming over here," Christina chuckled.

Trequan and Kaiden chuckled.

"Babe let's start to head out. We have a long drive ahead of us," Trequan said to Christina.

"Okay, babe," she remarked. "Isaias," she called.

Isaias and Kailyn walked over to the group.

"Yes, Mommy?"

"Tell Kaiden and Auntie Sam goodbye," she started, "we're about to head out babe."

Isaias looked at Kaiden and Kaiden squatted to be eye level with the child.

Isaias gave Kaiden a warm embrace.

"I had fun," he smiled.

"I'm glad, little man," Kaiden replied.

"Does this mean you and Auntie Sam are related now?" Isaias asked innocently.

The adults laughed.

"Yeah, man," Kaiden started. "She's my wife now. Which means, she's part of me." Kaiden touched his heart.

"So, she was your girlfriend before?" he asked.

Kaiden chuckled.

"Yeah, buddy. That's how it works. When two people really like each other, they are boyfriend and girlfriend," he looked at Christina and Trequan with a smile. "And then, when they love each other," he returned his attention to Isaias, "they become husband and wife, like Auntie Sam and I."

"Oh, I get it," Isaias spoke.

"Between you and me," Kaiden spoke in a low tone, "you may have to be the ring bearer again very soon for mommy and Tre," he chuckled.

Trequan overheard Kaiden and chuckled at his comment.

"What's next, Kai-G?" Trequan interjected.

"Honeymoon," Kaiden answered immediately. "Sam and I are setting off to see seven countries in two months."

Kaiden rose to his feet and took Samantha's hand. He picked up Kailyn in his free arm.

The group walked towards the exit.

"You all are going to be moving fast," Christina replied.

"Very fast," Samantha responded.

Kaiden kissed her on the cheek.

"She's been talking about seeing the world, so we're going to see as much as we can, as quickly as possible."

"What about *King Pin*?" Christina asked.

"The team is going to hold it down in my absence," Kaiden answered. "I trust that they can manage," he finished.

Trequan unlocked the car door and walked over to open Isaias' door.

Isaias hugged Kaiden. He embraced Samantha and she kissed him on the cheek.

"Bye Kailyn," he spoke to her.

Kailyn waved to Isaias.

"Bye Isay," she replied as she had difficulties pronouncing his full name.

"Bye Auntie Sam and Kaiden," Isaias spoke. "Have fun on your trip."

Kaiden and Samantha smiled.

"We'll see you soon, buddy," Kaiden replied.

Isaias got in the vehicle and Trequan closed the door.

Christina gave Samantha an embrace.

"Thanks, girl," Christina spoke.

Samantha smiled and gave Christina a nod.

"No need to thank me, girly," she knew why Christina was thanking her. "We're sisters."

Samantha kissed Christina on the cheek.

"Be safe," Christina added before she released her embrace with Samantha. "And congratulations again."

Christina walked over to Kaiden and looked at him.

He smiled at her.

She gave him a warm embrace.

As she hugged him, she was overwhelmed with flashbacks of their relationship; Kaiden experienced these flashbacks as well.

One flashback, they shared simultaneously.

***

"I'm going to always be in your life, Tina," Kaiden spoke.

"I hope so," Christina replied. "I would hate to lose you."

"You won't. Just don't do anything that may jeopardize us," he responded. "But as long as that doesn't happen, no matter where you go, near or far, I'll be there for you."

"Promise you won't let go?" she responded.

"I won't let go," Kaiden smirked.

Christina shed a tear as Kaiden spoke.

He leaned in and kissed her passionately.

***

"Thank you for everything, Kai," Christina whispered.

Kaiden chuckled lightly.

"I've prepared you for what you have now," he responded. "You have a good thing," Kaiden added.

"It's funny. Your wife told me the same thing earlier," Christina chuckled.

"Then, it must be true," Kaiden addressed. "Don't let anything interfere with what you have."

"I won't," Christina replied.

She kissed Kaiden on the cheek.

They both knew everything was dissolved between them but couldn't help but experience these moments when the two connected.

Kaiden kept his arm around Samantha.

Christina touched Kailyn's hair.

"Bye, baby," she spoke to Kailyn in a baby voice.

Kailyn chuckled at Christina.

"Bye, Auntie Tina," she smiled.

Christina teared up lightly as she turned to walk to her car.

Trequan helped her get in the passenger seat and put on her seatbelt.

He closed the door and she lowered the window.

Trequan walked over and embraced Samantha before giving Kaiden a firm handshake.

"Remember what I told you, man," Kaiden told him.

"I got you, bro," Trequan responded.

The handshake turned into an embrace.

Trequan walked to the driver's side and climbed inside.

"Christina," Kaiden called.

Christina looked out of the window and looked at Kaiden.

"Yeah?"

"Take care of yourself," he finished with a smile.

Christina smiled.

"You too, Kaiden."

www.ingramcontent.com/pod-product-compliance
Lightning Source LLC
Chambersburg PA
CBHW020640180626
46816CB00003B/1054

* 9 7 8 1 9 5 3 6 6 8 0 4 2 *